BYSTLE VALE

Mallet looked up into the face of the full moon, balled his right hand into a fist and smote his chest; a warrior's salute of respect and a call to war. A war he had no chance to win, but a war he would fight, oh yes, he would fight. Hopefully, Brynn, Cael and Needle would have the good sense to get the hells out of here before it was too late.

BYSTLE VALE
Cult of Yex Saga: Part III

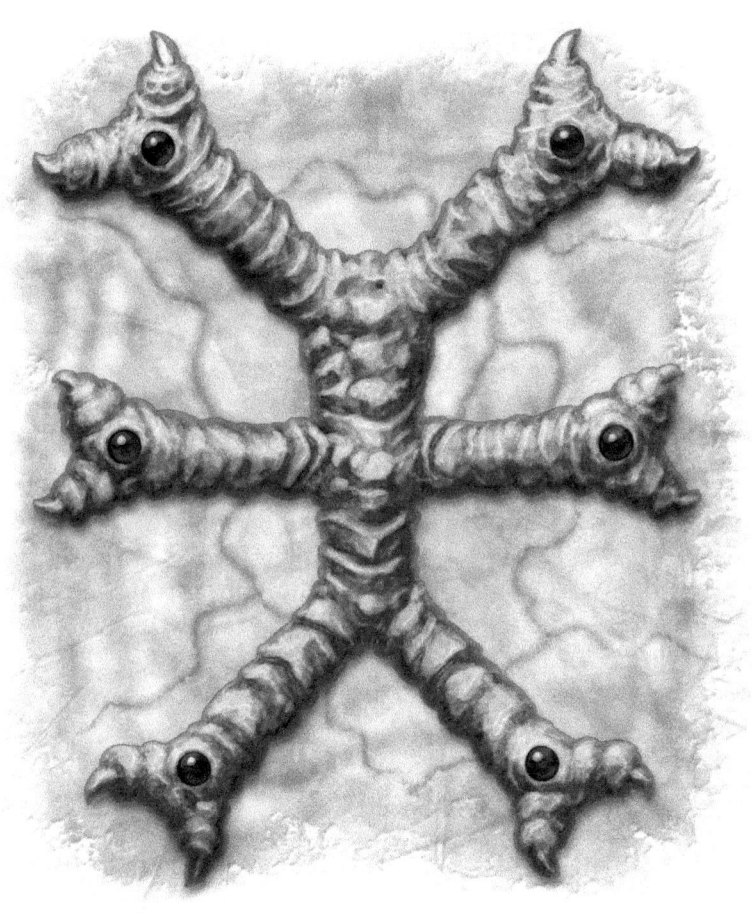

Jason F. Smith & C. Parker Garlitz
www.cultofyex.com

The Cult of Yex Saga Part III: Bystle Vale

Published by Taglyon Press, LLC

Cover Design by Brad Moulton

Proofreading: Jennifer Leigh

Cult of Yex Symbol Concept by Joseph Archer

Cult of Yex Symbol Illustration by Michael Philippi

ISBN 978-0-9862582-7-5

First Edition: September 2015

We dedicate this book to all the great fantasy authors we have loved over the years.

Bystle Vale is the third book of the Cult of Yex Saga. It is the continuation of the story that began in the first two books: Second Cataclysm, and Prophecies of Old. If you have not read the prior books in the series, we recommend you read them first before moving on to this one.

TABLE OF CONTENTS

PROLOGUE

"It is said that one man saved the world in ancient times. During the darkest hours when it seemed certain that the Cult of Yex would emerge victorious, Adirak, Wizard of Taglyon, stood strong. His unflinching leadership crushed the Cult and his cunning tactics imprisoned the great demon himself in the astral realm.

Adirak was crowned King of Taglyon. He spent his reign vanquishing remnants of the cult and establishing safeguards to ensure that its pernicious evil could never rise again. Despite his efforts, Adirak feared that a residue had somehow managed to elude him, awaiting a time of rebirth. But nary was a whisper heard from the Cult for thousands of years. But for the occasional rambling prophecies of madmen, the Cult was almost forgotten and the few who feared resurgence grew complacent.

If Adirak had lived a thousand lifetimes, he never could have predicted the manner in which the Cult had hidden itself. In his most fevered dreams he could not have imagined the demonic arcana that abetted them, nor their patient scheme to rise again and unleash their demon master."

-Prologue to the as yet unwritten Return of the Cult of Yex, by Caed the Chronicler

CHAPTER ONE
The Tower of Rovule

"At Xylex's direction, the Cult of Yex looted many of the finest treasures in the kingdoms of the ancient world. It was rumored that Xylex himself spent endless hours lording over the hoard that the cult had amassed. In the years following the fall of the Cult of Yex, Adirak spent untold resources hunting for the lost treasure, but he never found it."

- Caed The Chronicler

14th Day of Summer - 9:00 PM – The Nearly Full Moon – 24 Hours Until the Full Moon

Needle hunkered in the stern of the *Riparian Scout;* squinting downriver into the shadows slipping to their nightly rest. Mosquitos skittered on the burbling water, fair prey to the swooping bats that began darting down from their daytime roosts in small hollows on the gorge walls.

He's out there, Needle thought. *I don't care what Danilus says about how fast this boat goes up this river; Elija is out there following us. He is somehow swimming up the river and one night he's going to creep aboard and that massive spider hand is going to rip my insides out.* Needle imagined his guts being spooled around Elija's arm as the murderer stared down into Needle's dying eyes, a huge smile smeared across his face.

He shook his head. Son of Abyss, had he ever been this scared? In all the dusty trap-laden tombs he and his father had discovered and plundered, he had never felt this much terror. He hadn't slept well and when he was able to finally fall into troubled dozing, Elija haunted his dreams. Needle rarely left the stern of the boat since they'd made their escape from the Shrine of Ophidia three days ago.

What was that? Had he just seen something in the water or was it just another swallow diving for a late evening meal?

He squinted harder. It was too dark to see anything clearly. Darkness... he hated the darkness. That's when Elija would come...

Needle remembered the horrific Shrine of Ophidia. Elija, augmented by the venomous sigils, had broken the bonds of the undead snakes holding him. He remembered the snapping sound as the snakes were rent apart and the squeal of metal as Elija wrenched the chair free. Needle could feel the hair on the back of his neck rise again, hearing in his mind the scraping of metal across stone as Elija dragged the chair. And then the concussive crack as he hurled it against the crystal.

"No way he got out of there," Danilus said after they had fled the Shrine of Ophidia into the cavern and raced pell-mell through the narrow tunnel back out into the afternoon sun. They hadn't stopped there, but ran straight from the secret door in the stone cliff face to the *Riparian Scout*. Needle had kept a lookout as the others hastily threw the scattered supplies into the boat and Danilus pushed it away into the flow of the Demon River.

"He's not following," said Mallet, standing behind Needle. "Relax!"

But Needle did *not* relax as the sail popped in the wind and they lurched northward through the mouth of the gorge.

And three days later, he could still hear that awful sound of the metal chair as Elija hurled it against the 'unbreakable' window.

No... Elija had escaped. Needle was sure of it. He'd seen the crack inching through the crystal. He'd seen the massive muscles that enhanced the monster. There was no way that prison could hold him.

He is out there... hells bent on murder.

The night air was crisp as Mallet stood at the prow of the *Riparian Scout* desperately searching the sky for a hint of the rising moon. The others seemed more worried about whether Elija was stalking them, but not Mallet. His primary concern was in the sky. Tomorrow night the moon would be full.

He could see its faint light in the few wispy clouds above him, but at this moment, the orb of his doom still lay hidden behind the gorge walls that chambered the Demon River. He could taste Wheizer's blood in the back of his throat again, and simultaneously felt a phantom stab of pain deep in his shoulder.

So many conflicting thoughts and emotions swirled within him. He doubted his own judgment and longed to talk to his father. His father... He had forced himself not to even think of Dagorn's actions. The emotional pain of his father's betrayal had been worse than the wounds inflicted by Wheizer in the mausoleum, but the worry of the nearly full moon made it impossible to ignore the question any longer. He had not allowed himself to ask... *Why would a father infect his own son with the wererat disease like that?*

No matter how he tried, he couldn't imagine why his father... any father... would allow such a thing to happen to his son. The sense of abandonment and betrayal was...

He looked skyward again to the moon to prevent a welling tear from spilling down his cheek.

He had always relied on his father's counsel, but something had changed since the fateful night that his mother had been murdered by the Agrabi intruder. His father had grown distant and cold. Mallet had always attributed it to his father's grief. But wouldn't a father turn to his children at a time of grieving? Dagorn had not. However, in light of what his father had done to him, it seemed his coldness was beyond grief. A year of his father's growing emotional distance had culminated with that black night when his father had made Wheizer infect him. Perhaps his father was punishing him? It had been the same day he killed Vosc at the docks. Perhaps, in his disappointment, Dagorn had lashed out?

He wanted so badly to talk with someone... discuss his worries. With his mother gone, who else could he turn to? The wicked secrets his mother harbored had spread to his sister. Brynn was now embracing them with zeal. He felt utterly alone.

He chastised himself. Such weak thoughts were for children and women. There was no one to turn to but himself, and there never would be again. His father had betrayed him and in some sense so had his mother and his sister. He was on a different path now, with Cael. *If, of course, I don't shift tomorrow night and end up killing everyone.*

He thought again of the day he had killed Vosc at the docks. He gripped the haft of his glaive with one hand and ran his other hand over the smooth skin of his freshly shorn scalp. His chest was still a little sore from the wounds Wheizer had given him, but had healed remarkably well. Danilus had said that the lycanthropy had helped him to heal quickly. Wheizer's poison was both a bane and a boon...

But Wheizer wasn't the real enemy right now. The real adversary was Mallet himself... and the monstrous Elija. What might Mallet do to his friends tomorrow night when the white light of the full moon freed his inner butcher?

The logical thing to do would be to just flee. Go off on his own, to spare his sister and his companions of the berserk wererat rampage. That would save them. But Elija was still out there. Without him, Elija would leave them no less dead. He couldn't run away and he couldn't stay.

Perhaps fate would allow his first wererat shifting to coincide with their next encounter with Elija... It might take a wererat to finally kill that monster. Perhaps such a situation would save his companions? He clung desperately to that slim hope.

He had battled Elija twice now: once at the swamp tree with Danilus and Dheke, then again in the horrible shrine... but that was before the abominable witch marks had turned him into a much more powerful foe. The others dreaded another fight with Elija but Mallet longed for it. He could feel the battle-lust building inside him. Did that feeling come from him? After all, hadn't he killed two men in cold blood? Or was it the wererat poison?

As they rounded a bend in the river, the nearly full moon hove into view and Mallet knew which answer he feared most.

Danilus stood at the tiller under the full sail, guiding them slowly up the canyon. Cael dozed in a hammock in the cabin. Mallet seethed as he watched his sister.

Brynn sat at a makeshift table on the deck, a lantern providing illumination for her work. The damnable book filled with witch marks lay open on the table as she scratched a pattern into the surface of the flat rock she had so carefully chosen from the shore. Needle sat across from her, gnawing on a piece of jerky as he watched her while occasionally glancing back downriver.

Mallet wanted to grab the lot of it and hurl it into the river like he'd tried to do earlier on the trip. But he looked up at the moon and the uncertainty of tomorrow kept him quiet. He did not want an argument to be the last thing either of them remembered about each other if the worst should happen.

"Yeah, but how does it work?" Needle asked for the umpteenth time.

"It just does. Needle," Brynn said in exasperation. "I trace the pattern and it will light up."

"But where does the light come from?" Needle asked.

Brynn just ignored him and held the stone next to a page in her book, comparing the patterns to make sure they were the same. Satisfied, she reached for some ink. She carefully brushed several coats of the purplish stain into the depressions she'd carved on the stone, then held it up to the warmth of the lantern to dry.

"It's the same sigil I drew in the sand on the floor of the Mausoleum in Demon's bluff," Brynn finally said.

From his vantage, Mallet could see the outline of the wicked pattern curving along the surface of the flat rock. It wouldn't take any effort at all to snatch it away from his sister and hurl it into the water.

"So do it," Needle urged as Brynn admired her handiwork. "I bet it doesn't work."

A bleary-eyed Cael emerged from the cabin. "Can't sleep."

"Me neither," Mallet said, glancing at the moon again.

Brynn laid her index finger in the center of the pattern on the stone and slowly traced it. Needle, fascinated, leaned in close to watch.

Mallet smiled as Needle lurched back when the stone lit up in a searing, bluish light. His worries prevented him from laughing out loud like the moment deserved.

Brynn quickly reversed the trace on the stone and it went dark.

"Holy hells," Needle breathed. "You can turn it off, too?"

"On and off," Brynn said. "Like lighting and extinguishing this lantern."

"What if I trace it?" Needle asked very much the fascinated child. "Can I?" he pleaded.

Mallet sat fuming as he watched his sister indoctrinate the little runt with her poisonous craft. Needle tried in futility to trace the pattern again and again. Brynn nearly gave up on him before he finally managed to light the thing.

Mallet watched on in disgust. Like a toddler with a new toy, Needle delightedly traced the pattern over and over, lighting and darkening the stone, until Mallet couldn't watch anymore. He nearly snatched the filthy stone away from Needle but decided to return to the prow of the boat and his troubled thoughts.

14th Day of Summer – 5:00 AM – The Switchback Trail – 17 Hours Until the Full Moon

"Ho! There it is!" Danilus called from the wheel of the *Riparian Scout*. Mallet, still in the prow, looked up at the gargantuan dam several hundred yards upriver: the towering edifice was bathed in the residual light of the early morning moon in the west. Everyone knew that there was a dam far to the north of Demon's Bluff that helped to regulate the seasonal flooding of the Demon River, but Mallet had never seen it. It was ancient. Some even said it was built by the dwarves in a time before the cult. Mallet marveled at how incredibly *old* it felt.

The black basalt soared in a smooth curve from the bottom of the gorge all the way to the crenelated top; a seemingly impenetrable wall of darkness. It reminded Mallet of a fortress with battlements and ramparts.

Danilus steered the boat to starboard and beached it on long stretch of sand on the eastern bank. A thicket of willow brush grew at the base of the gorge where the canyon walls met the sandy beach.

"Are we here?" asked Cael. "Toss that anchor on the beach, big fella," Danilus called to Mallet. It landed with a crunch on the pebbles of the embankment.

Danilus pointed to the eastern wall of the canyon with his chin. "I reckon it's too dark yet to see," he said leaping over the side onto the beach. "But behind them willows is the start of a trail up that canyon wall. It switchbacks all the way up. Hells of a climb, I tell ya. I gone up it when I was a lad." Dheke, Boxxaway's old mastiff, leaped onto the sandy beach and immediately began sniffing around.

"What do you mean?" asked Needle.

"This is the place," said Danilus. "Boxxaway told me to drop you here. I reckon you'll get to the top about sunup. Then head east into the rising sun, and I reckon you'll find that king and his vale soon enough."

Brynn stepped out of the cabin.

"Go up now?" Cael asked, as he threaded a scabbard onto his belt. "While it's still dark?" He slid the dagger into it, pausing for a moment to stare at the blade; it was the dagger Danilus had given him from his grandfather. *The dagger that killed my parents...*

"What about the third orb?" Needle asked.

"I was able to see it in the distance from back where Elija destroyed the last one," said Brynn. "It's up there on the escarpment somewhere."

"Shouldn't you paint that sigil back on?" Needle asked. Mallet had been relieved when she had finally washed the mark off of her forehead after they had raced back to the boat and resumed their journey upriver.

"I can always put it back if needed," said Brynn, patting her re-stocked satchel.

"Sooner you get going the better, I reckon," said Danilus. "Especially if you want stay ahead of that creature. I don't expect he stops to sleep."

Mallet stared up the high canyon wall. His fate lay somewhere up there. Tomorrow night's full moon was inevitable. "What if the Elija creature is up there already?" he asked. If a flush of excitement showed on his face, it was veiled by the darkness.

"We have to be ahead of him, don't we?" Brynn asked, giving him a stern look. She nodded her head slightly toward Needle.

"I saw that," Needle said. "He's out there somewhere... I can feel it!"

Mallet hated to agree with Needle, but.... He had a weird feeling that the little mutated whore had somehow managed to get ahead of them again.

Mallet hopped over the rail, his boots crunching on the pebbles and sand of the bank.

"So without Brynn's sigil, how do we find the orb up there?" Needle asked.

"I have the *Lorgnettes* with me," said Cael, patting a pocket in his robe.

"Get going," Danilus urged, making a scooting motion.

"Wait a minute," said Needle as he disembarked. "You're not coming with us?"

"This falls to you four," Danilus said. "'Sides, I don't think ol' Boxxaway intended for me go along and I got a few things to keep me busy."

"But what about the creature?" Needle asked desperately, a squeak making its way into his voice. "What if he is behind us?"

"Don't worry, Needle," Mallet said, slapping the bony boy on the back. "I got you covered!" He spun his glaive so the cold steel glinted in the lantern light.

"I reckon us sitting here guarding your backside is what old Dheke and I will do," Danilus added.

"But that's crazy!" Needle cried. "You wouldn't stand a chance against him alone!"

"I got Dheke," Danilus said, suddenly very serious. "I don't know if you noticed or not, but that fella don't cotton too much to ol' Dheke. You go on up, and worry about what you got to worry about. We'll be fine right here. 'Sides," he winked. "I betcha there are some big ol' bonebacks in the deep water at the base of that dam."

Mallet led the way up the switchback trail. His sister followed a few dozen feet behind. Cael and Needle hiked together ten yards behind her. He heard bits of their low conversation; Needle's voice especially was prone to carry.

Mallet heard words like 'full moon' and 'rat out' and 'not much time' and 'silver dagger'. Needle had threatened him directly more than once over the wererat concern.

Mallet was surprised—it should be making him angry, but it wasn't. How could he blame Needle? No way was the little guy ever going to trust a wererat. After all, hadn't Wheizer murdered his mother?

"Do you hear that?" Brynn asked.

"Yeah, I hear them," Mallet replied.

"No," Brynn said. "It's a sound like rushing water."

"The river, I expect."

"No, it's different than that. It gets clearer the higher we get."

"Not sure," Mallet said. "Probably just a trick of the canyon." He kept hiking. He distinctly heard Needle mention his silver dagger again...

15ᵗʰ Day of Summer - 6:45 AM – Scouts– About 15 Hours Until the Full Moon

It was daybreak as Rathenel's scout watched the escarpment. Four young humans suddenly emerged where the switchback trail met the top of the cliff. There were three males and a female. All four were very tall, but one was impossibly large and bald-headed. He'd hate to have to fight such a giant. The four of them turned and looked out over the gorge, talking to one another. Rathenel had given strict instructions to report immediately if he should spot them. Tharchelon would want to know they were here and would probably come to greet them very shortly.

The Rothkin scout slunk back into the underbrush, unseen by the four.

Mallet reached the top and despite a lingering burn in his thighs, he felt good. The sun was still below the tree line in the east but the western top of the cliff was brightening in the morning light.

"You guys got to look at this," Needle said in an awed voice, standing on the edge of the gorge. Mallet joined him. *A quick shove could send him flying to his death.*

Mallet shook his head and sighed. Why did such thoughts enter his mind? Was it the wererat venom?

He looked over the precipice with Needle. The view was indeed impressive. From this vantage, he could see the dam, the reservoir behind it and a spectacular view of the gorge below. The plateau on both sides of the gorge was lined with pine trees, and the air had an incredible, cool, fresh smell that was altogether unfamiliar to him.

"Look," said Brynn, pointing to the dam. The morning light clearly revealed a crack halfway up the dam. Water gushed out in a spray that cascaded down, darkening the stone over which it ran. "I knew I heard something!"

"That doesn't look right at all," Needle whistled. "Is that new, or has it been going on for a while?"

"Not sure," said Cael. "Do you think maybe the earthquake reached this far north? And cracked the dam?"

"Look over there," Brynn said pointing across to the other side of the gorge. Mallet spotted it right away. There was a section of the far canyon wall that had broken away from the cliff face. Trees leaned over the cliff at odd angles, and a large rubble pile at the bottom of the cliff told the tale. There was no doubt that the landslide was recent. "There's your answer," Needle said. "We missed that rubble pile in the dark last night as we sailed past."

"But look at that!" Cael exclaimed, looking the other direction, turning them all around. From where they stood at the edge of the cliff, a trail forked east and south into a grove of conifers. The trail to the south disappeared into gloomy darkness, but the trail to the east led past a huge and badly weatherworn obelisk. Beyond that, visible through the pines, was a crumbling stone tower. Both the obelisk and tower looked incredibly old. The top portion of the tower had collapsed and stone blocks and rubble lay scattered about. The air was pierced by the sudden cry of a hawk in the distance.

"Holy Hells!" Needle breathed as he began walking east toward the tower. Mallet followed him, giving a last lingering look at the crack in the dam. He had the unsettling feeling that someone was watching them.

"Do you know what this is?" Needle asked excitedly, after winding along the path toward the obelisk and the tower. He didn't wait for them to guess. "This is the Tower of Rovule!"

"*And?*" Brynn said with a hint of exasperation.

"My father told me about it," said Needle. "He came here once. Ages ago, the Cult of Yex kept a huge treasure hoard here. This tower was filled with art and golden statuettes and gem encrusted goblets and, and... so much gold you would never worry about food again! Stuff they stole during their rise to power. It was all here once."

"What happened to it?" Mallet asked.

"Nobody knows. It all disappeared eons ago." Needle said. "My father used to daydream about finding the lost cache. It's every treasure hunter's dream. He came here once when he was a boy. He said this tower was picked clean. Nothing left here at all."

"Hmff," Mallet said. "Shouldn't we get about finding the orb and moving east?"

Needle was ahead of them, about to pass the obelisk, when

several dozen starlings suddenly burst forth from the openings in the tower. *What in the hells? Something is not right*, Mallet thought. He felt a sudden surge of giddy anticipation. He gripped his glaive and filled his lungs with the strange sap-tinged smell of the northern woods.

Elija Abel, ensigiled, muscled and augmented with protruding knife-sharp bones, stepped from an archway at the base of the tower. Between two fingers of his normal left hand, he held the third black orb. His monstrous deformed right hand hung limp at his side, the long, jointed spider fingers twitching.

His face was expressionless despite being covered by the swirling witch marks, but Mallet could sense the smile in his dead, reddish eyes when their gaze met.

Needle backpedaled as Elija started to approach them. Everything had gone silent for Mallet except for the sound of his hand stretching and gripping the haft of his glaive.

Every nerve tingled fire, but his heart seemed to stop in mid-beat. Colors got brighter. He could smell his own sweat mingle with the aroma of leather, pine needles, and the tint of oiled steel from the blade of his glaive. Suddenly, contrary to the clarity he was feeling, his head began to spin. His legs wobbled.

What in the hells was happening?

An ear-splitting crack shattered the morning air, followed by a massive peal of thunder. The earth heaved, causing the pine trees to sway unnaturally. *Another earthquake?*

Even Elija looked confused and unsure. He hunkered slightly to stabilize himself, his hand gripping the orb tightly as he struggled to stay standing.

Needle stopped his back-pedaling right in front of Mallet. The little Agrabi seemed unaffected by the roiling waves of earth, moving with a strange grace and alacrity.

Needle grunted, a deep guttural sound that seemed impossible from his scrawny frame and raced forward directly at Elija. Mallet watched slack-jawed. Needle... cowardly... whiny... complaining Needle charged straight toward the doom of Elija Abel.

What happened next seemed to occur in slow motion. Mallet noticed that the obelisk was beginning to topple.

Elija hunkered further to take Needle's charge. The little Agrabi slammed into him and bounced backwards, falling on his backside. But he had knocked Elija back... one fateful step.

WHAM!

The huge obelisk crushed the vile monster. Only his head, left shoulder and arm escaped the direct impact.

The ground kept shaking, finally knocking Mallet down, but he felt a rush of exultation nevertheless. If anything could have killed the bulgy little bastard, it was that falling obelisk. *And Needle!* The scrawny Agrabi son of Abyss was full of surprises!

Needle stood back up, seemingly impervious to the jitter and dance of the ground.

That ground shook for a few more moments, then began to stabilize, though the thunderous sound continued. Mallet stood and approached the fallen rock, his glaive held out before him.

Elija was alive, but utterly pinned. He cursed in an unknown language. Black froth flecked his pale lips. His chest, legs, and spidery right hand were crushed under the block of stone. Black ichor pooled at the stone's edge.

The black orb lay on the ground next to him. He had dropped it but didn't seem to care. He used his unpinned hand in an effort to lift the stone.

To Mallet's amazement, he was actually moving the obelisk! The creature was impossibly strong.

Cael scooted past Mallet and picked up the orb, then backed away quickly.

"Now what?" Needle asked.

Mallet grimaced and answered by swinging his glaive down at the trapped creature's skull. *Thunk.* Like a dull axe against hard wood, the blade cut the skin of his head, but stopped short at the bone of his skull.

"By the whores of hells," Mallet swore.

"He's all hopped up on those sigils," Needle almost shouted.

The air seemed suddenly humid and smelled moldy. If they didn't do something, Elija was going to push the stone off himself in a just few minutes, no matter how wounded he was.

Elija lifted the stone an inch... Mallet jumped on top of the stone, causing it to fall back onto Elija.

"Cael," shouted Brynn, "Some magic here! Fire. Destruction. Wizard stuff!"

Cael took a deep breath and closed his eyes. Why was he taking so long? A small shaft of bright light beamed from his pointed finger and struck Elija on the face. Elija flinched as the eldritch dart struck him but he continued to struggle to lift the block.

Mallet stabbed down from his position on top of the stone with his glaive, doing very little damage, but at least preventing Elija from throwing off the stone.

A wind sucked through the trees and the branches swayed, allowing patterns of sunlight to dapple the ground at their feet. Taking a deep breath, Mallet continued to stab downward, though his shoulders ached from the effort.

Elija reacted in a sudden rush of squirming. Perhaps his glaive was finally doing some damage? Cael prepared another spell. Needle looked over to the trees, then back at Elija, staring in wonderment.

"Do something!" Mallet hissed to him. "Your silver dagger!" He couldn't keep this up forever. Elija made a supreme effort and manage to slide the rock a few inches. Mallet struggled to keep his feet and renewed his flurry of blows against the bony creature. He enjoyed a fight more than most, but it was clear that Elija would eventually free himself. Everyone had been worried about the full moon tonight, but it suddenly seemed unlikely he would live to see it.

Needle turned and raced about thirty feet east toward a large pine tree; it was one of the few that grew in the clearing. It cast its long early morning shadow over them. Like a monkey, Needle began to climb straight up, weaving skillfully through the branches.

"What in the infernal hells are you doing?" Mallet roared.

Needle ignored him and kept climbing. About a quarter of the way up, he stopped and stared at something, his face contorted into a puzzled expression. He shook his head and kept climbing.

The stone began to lift. "Needle!" Mallet screamed again.

The breeze was gone, replaced only with sticky-sweet humidity. A deep rumble vibrated the ground and the hairs on his arms. His beating heart echoed in his ears, thrumming with a faster and faster cadence.

Needle stood on a solid-looking branch and started walking out on it.

"What in the name of the Abyss are you doing?" Mallet screamed.

Panic, a new sensation, filled him. Elija, with his crushed spider-hand, had lifted the stone enough that he was starting to crawl out. Mallet stabbed madly to no effect. Another thin ray of fire from Cael made the monster flinch but not much more.

Brynn threw a rock, which bounced off Elija's head. *What else did he expect from a girl*, Mallet thought.

Needle balanced his way out on to the branch. He took hold of another branch and started to lift. He strained as he finally gained enough leverage on the bough to begin to lift it above his head. The branch creaked and cracked at the strain. A beam of morning sunlight broke through where Needle had cleared its path. The yellow light illuminated the fallen obelisk. In that moment, Elija was fully exposed to the sun.

"No..." was all Mallet could say, suddenly frozen.

As the sunlight struck Elija directly, something began to happen to him. He stiffened, and the large stone began to weigh down upon him again. His coloration began to change: his dark hair began to lighten, his pale skin began to darken. It was as if all Elija's colors began to drift to their opposite.

Never in the short time Mallet had battled Elija had he seen the slightest trace of emotion on the undead creature's face, until now. Anger? Rage? Confusion?

No... it was *fear*.

Needle made a supreme effort, lifting the branch even higher, further baptizing Elija in the morning sun. The creature let out a gravelly, ethereal scream of terror and rage. Mallet squinted as Elija suddenly seemed to separate into two distinct figures, one with proper color and the other with opposite colors. Mallet immediately feared they had just doubled their problems, but as swiftly as Elija had separated into two distinct entities, he just as quickly recombined.

Mallet cringed as the two forms impacted and exploded in a burst of whirling shadows. He was blasted backwards off the stone, landing with a 'wuff.' Cael and Brynn were also knocked back by the explosion. The shadows whirled in an insane dance. Blackish tendrils reached in all directions and then faded into nothingness like smoke on the wind.

Mallet heaved himself onto his feet, and jumped on top of the fallen stone.

Elija Abel was gone. Not a single trace remained...

"HA!" Needle hooted as he climbed down the tree. "Did you *see* that?"

"What did you do?"

Needle dropped to the ground with a grin. "I'll be damned and doubled damned... that was the most amazing thing I've ever seen in my life!"

"How did you know the light would hurt him?" asked Mallet in awe.

"Hey!" said Brynn, interrupting him. "Listen!"

The thundering sound he heard at the beginning of the earthquake was still going, but now it was growing louder and louder.

Cael ran back along the path toward the edge of the gorge. Mallet reached down, picked up a still prone Brynn and followed.

"Hells," Cael shouted as he reached the edge of the gorge. His voice warbled with terror.

Mallet arrived, propelling Brynn. Needle somehow had reached the edge first. Mallet looked over the smaller boy's shoulder.

"Hells is right..." Mallet breathed.

"It's gone..." Needle whispered.

"Danilus..." Cael croaked, his voice lost.

The dam was gone... entirely. The lake was still funneling down the gorge in a white frothy roar, tossing tree trunks and boulders like they were sticks and pebbles.

All of their heads turned south, down the gorge toward Demon's Bluff. "There is no way to warn them," Needle said, his voice broken.

CHAPTER TWO
Out of the Emptiness... Salvation!

"No point in giving up. Every problem has a solution... keep looking."

- Mogwar Von Torinovo

15th Day of Summer – 7:00 AM – Eastern Plateau – 15 Hours Until the Full Moon

Tharchelon arrived with his small retinue at the ancient ruins of the tower by the gorge. He watched with relief from the edge of the clearing, hidden in a thicket of scrub oak as the obelisk toppled over and crushed Elija Abel.

The thunderclap and earthquake were deeply worrying, but his primary focus was the status of the children. He welcomed the relief he felt to see that indeed they had survived. He badly needed those children alive, as they were the linchpin of his new plan...

The fact that Elija fought to free himself from under the huge stone gave Tharchelon great consternation, and he dug his dirty fingernails into his palms with excruciating anxiety as he watched. They flailed away at him until he finally expired in a puff of black smoke. He needn't have worried.

These children were more resourceful than they looked. He reminded himself not to forget that he mustn't underestimate them.

The back of his tongue still ached for the taste of the moss, but at least the itching had stopped and his headache was finally diminishing. His wrist, fingers and ribs were healing and best of all, he once again had his wits about him, though not without considerable mental effort. The moss pangs had been his constant companion since he had regained consciousness back at the exile camp. He dared to hope that his new plan would work, especially since the children had survived, but he couldn't shake a stubborn sense of despair. In order to keep his spirits up, he tried to keep his mind away from his awful situation, instead replaying in his mind the plan he had formulated yesterday.

14th Day of Summer - 7:00 AM – Solutions – 36 Hours until the Full Moon

Tharchelon woke as the morning sunlight peeked between the boughs of his lean-to. His soup spooning benefactor was nowhere to be seen. He took a deep breath, his mouth filled with a rush of sour saliva. A pinch of the Bystle Moss would taste perfect right now, but it was the moss that had caused his pain. Because of it, he had endured this hellish nightmare and suffering... he endured it still. He had lost everything. His kingdom... gone. His warm bed, his throne, his library. Gone. All gone. He had been exiled by his own people; sneezed unceremoniously from his kingdom. He was denied any return to his home and his moss.

Weak and shaky, Tharchelon crawled out of the lean-to. The near full moon was barely visible in the growing light of the morning. The camp was littered with makeshift shelters. Most were pine bough lean-tos like the one from which he had just emerged, but some were larger shelters covered with animal skins or tarps. Cook fires smoked here and there as ragged-looking Rothkin began to mill about the makeshift camp.

The babbling of running water reached his ears from off to the right where the trees were dense. It gave him a sense of location, as the stream was familiar to him from the hunting trips of his youth. The stream flowed west to dump its tribute into the reservoir. Their camp was somewhere downstream of the very same brook that cut through the northern end of the Bystle Vale. He breathed in deeply through his nose and filled his lungs, despite the lingering soreness of his cracked ribs. The air was crisp and smelled of pine sap and smoke. It made him long for autumn, his favorite season, though that was still months away.

He stood, allowing his eyes to adjust to the light. To his amazement, his adjutant Rathenel approached out of nowhere. "My King! You are up!"

Tharchelon scowled, "How are you here?"

Rathenel frowned, "We've been tending to you!"

"You and the old woman?"

"Others as well."

Tharchelon wondered what just a little pinch of moss might taste like right now, absently feeling for his pockets. Curse Nelcherath and his putrid soul to the Abyss for eternity! "If you are here, you are trapped outside that infernal barrier like I am," he said to his adjutant.

Rathenel nodded, "We all are, my King. We were also exiled because of our loyalty to you."

"And we have no way of getting back to the moss garden," Tharchelon went on absently.

"The moss garden?"

Tharchelon caught himself, "That is my sacred duty, as King, to protect it... and our people. But Nelcherath has betrayed us. We can't go back."

"Ah. We should talk about that," Rathenel said, pointing off toward the center of the camp. "Do you see that large lodge?"

Tharchelon's head began to ache again as he squinted in the direction Nelcherath was pointing. His headache was nothing compared to those he had recently endured, but a bittersweet pinch of moss would solve it.

"Come, my King," said Rathenel as he started walking toward the center of the camp. "As you can see, many of your people remain loyal. As of my most recent count yesterday, we are just over 700 with more arriving each day."

They strolled past a cook fire surrounded by a family consisting of husband, wife and three young children. The woman tended a pot hung over the fire on a tripod. The parents recognized him and stood, then bowed as he and Rathenel walked by. Tharchelon acknowledged them with the slightest of nods. Rathenel continued, "As you can see there are many women and children, but among the exiles there are over 80 warriors, many from your palace guard."

Tharchelon's heart leapt upon hearing the number. "Why does Nelcherath exile them?"

"He fears anyone who was, is, or might be loyal to you. There are almost another 200 able-bodied men," Rathenel continued. "We have already begun to train them; though equipping them is more of a challenge."

"For what?" shot Tharchelon. He could hear the anger and despair in his own voice. "Nelcherath and his traitors cower like dogs behind that barrier."

The big lodge hove into clear view a few dozen yards hence. Word that he had recovered was racing through the camp, and people were beginning to follow him. Their whispers reminded him of the fateful night in the moss garden. It was reassuring to see so many familiar faces; all were filthy and unwashed, but many were smiling and some even streaked with tears of joy and relief. Tharchelon met their eyes and nodded as he and Rathenel walked. They approached the structure, a patchwork of pine boughs, tarps and deer hides. The familiar faces of two of his palace guards stood outside the flap that covered the opening.

Rathenel stopped before them and leaned in close to whisper. "My King, Thockenar the High Druid has been investigating the barrier and has some thoughts about it. We have not been idle."

The guards stepped aside as they entered, one holding open the flap for them.

A fire crackled at the center of the round lodge, its smoke rising through a hole in the domed ceiling. Four thick, upright pine logs provided the support. Thockenar, dressed in his customary green robes, paced with his arms folded within the sleeves. The Druid was old and stoic. Only hints of black remained in hair that had long gone gray. In all the years that Tharchelon had known the old Druid, he had never seen him smile.

It didn't take him long to imagine the reason for the old Druid being here, and it most certainly was not loyalty to him personally. Thockenar was loyal to some higher purpose that only he understood. The old Druid was nothing if not a firm adherent to orthodoxy. He used to flash dour frowns at the most minor deviations from established rituals and traditions.

Tharchelon intuited the most likely chain of events: Thockenar must have been vocal in his disapproval of Nelcherath's treachery, not for any impropriety to Tharchelon, but because it was an affront to established mores. So Nelcherath expelled him for it. Normally, Tharchelon would have driven himself to distraction over such a tenuous and impersonal rationale for loyalty. But under the current circumstances, he was simply grateful for the old Druid's presence.

Thockenar turned and bowed deeply as they entered. "I'm glad to see Your Highness is recovering."

Tharchelon nodded. Wouldn't a pinch of moss taste good right now? Calm his nerves? A rush of the bitter flavor on his tongue... maybe push it between his lip and gum and let the sensation course through him.

He jerked out of his fantasy. Damn hells, he needed to concentrate. "What news of the traitor?" he demanded.

"My sense is that he is frightened," Thockenar said without enthusiasm. "His actions were hasty and poorly planned. He finds himself in a position of power he did not expect and he lacks the... decisiveness that his situation requires."

"I fail to take your meaning."

"My King, Nelcherath is faced with a population that doubts his leadership, regardless of their... feelings for your reign. In the day following your departure, Nelcherath was confronted by the fact that many were not pleased with his actions. I think this caught him by surprise."

"His actions?" Tharchelon demanded. "You mean treason!"

"Ahh... yes. Treason."

Tharchelon's suspicions were confirmed. Thockenar was choosing his words carefully.

"Your Highness," Rathenel interjected, "I think the High Druid means to say that Nelcherath failed to take decisive action when a strong leader like you would not have hesitated."

"Indeed," Thockenar resumed his pacing. "When one commits treason, one must be prepared to follow through. Nelcherath should have put down the dissention with ruthless action; perhaps even a few public executions. But he lacks the stomach for it, so he began the expulsions instead."

"He has grown paranoid, my King," Rathenel said excitedly. "He orders exile for the slightest cause. His hold on power is tenuous. Every exile accrues to our advantage."

"Our advantage?" Tharchelon roared. "What advantage have we, when the traitor cowers behind his impenetrable magical wall?"

"Thockenar thinks it may not be so impenetrable after all, Highness," said Rathenel calmly. "As I said, we have not been idle."

"Indeed, I have spent much of the last days investigating the nature of this barrier, my King." Thockenar looked almost enthused now.

Tharchelon cut him off. "Let me tell you of *my* investigation!"

If Thockenar was irritated, he hid it completely behind his stoic façade.

"The barrier is as hard as stone," Tharchelon said. "It encircles the vale completely. It cannot be climbed over, nor dug under!"

"I can confirm all you say," said the High Druid, nonplussed. "I sat at the barrier for a day and observed."

"And?" Tharchelon demanded with a raised eyebrow and a low voice.

"I watched as a squirrel scampered through the underbrush and passed through the barrier into the vale. For the squirrel, it was as if there was no barrier at all."

Tharchelon was sure that he looked as confused as he felt.

"Then I myself walked to the barrier, but was stopped."

"I don't understand," said Tharchelon.

"Neither did I, Highness, so I continued to observe. Being mid-summer, I watched a nest of young sparrows in a branch some distance inside the barrier. They were stretching their wings to leave the nest for the first time. I watched as one of the sparrows flew out past the barrier to alight upon a pine branch near me. After a rest, it flew back to its mother's nest, but hit the barrier. I had to deal it mercy, as it was badly injured."

"So you killed a bird?" grated Tharchelon in growing frustration. "Is there a point to your prattle?"

"If I may interject, Highness," said Rathenel. "The point is that some creatures may pass through the barrier, while others may not."

Tharchelon blinked.

"I continued my observations and added some experiments throughout the day and I have developed a theory about the nature of the barrier," the old druid seemed to show a hint of excitement. "The Druids who stayed with Nelcherath tapped the magic of the Bystle Tree to erect the barrier."

The old Druid's words reminded Tharchelon of something his father once told him. The first of their people who came to the vale in ancient times had used the magic of the vale to erect a barrier that hid them from the rest of the world. It made the vale seem as if it were uninhabited and caused disinterest in any who approached so they would simply wander away. After a time it was deemed unnecessary and the protective barrier was taken down. *If only there was a way to take down Nelcherath's damnable barrier!*

"But I do not think Nelcherath's Druids understand the nature of that magic as I now do," Thockenar continued. "Where we find ourselves now... so distant from the vale, there is none of the magic in which we have lived our entire lives. I feel its absence acutely. Here, outside the vale, there is a sort of magic, but it is thin and foreign. It is not the same comforting magic that infuses the vale and all that live within it."

"And what does it all mean?" Tharchelon asked. He may not have felt the absence of magic, but damn hells; he most certainly missed his moss. He rubbed his tongue against the roof of his mouth, imagining again the bittersweet taste.

"I believe that the barrier can only block creatures that have previously lived in the presence of the vale's magic."

"It's why the squirrel that lived outside the vale could enter," said Rathenel excitedly. "But the bird that lived within it could not!"

"In other words, there is a flaw in the barrier that Nelcherath's Druids could not have foreseen," the old druid continued. "The barrier knows you. It knows *us*, my King. We have lived immersed in that magic which gives the barrier life. Because it *knows us*, it can keep us out."

Tharchelon was not following. His brain felt as if it was covered in a fog and he couldn't think fast enough.

"So if we find someone from outside to help us," said Rathenel with a broad grin. *"Someone who had never been in the vale before..."*

"They could walk right through the barrier and into the vale!" Thockenar finished.

A pinch of moss would clear his head and help him to think. Somewhere in the jabbering of his counselors, was the germ of an idea, but he could not follow it. Just a tiny taste would fix him right up. "But that doesn't solve the problem of getting *us* back into the vale!" He could hear the frustration in his own voice. "And even if it did, who do we get to go into the vale in the first place?"

Even as he said it, a thought came to him. His mind raced. The interlopers were likely already dead. He had made a bargain with the creature from the shadow dimension in the moss garden. Elija would hunt them down single-mindedly and kill them. *Perhaps they survived?* Maybe the visitor in dreams had somehow preserved them?

"Are there any other options?" Tharchelon asked.

"Well," said Rathenel, "There is old Chetelar."

"The lame beggar?" Tharchelon asked.

"He is still in the vale and he is loyal to you," Rathenel said.

"How do you know this?" Tharchelon asked. "That he is loyal?"

"One of the old women spoke with him through the barrier. He was wandering in the western end of the vale several nights ago and she called out to him. She brought me to him. He is loyal but he is terrified. I tried to convince him to simply attend court held by Nelcherath and bring us any news, but he refused. Fear is more crippling to him than his crooked leg."

"Coward," Tharchelon hissed. "Is he of no use at all?"

Thockenar cleared his throat. "You are correct, Highness; there is certainly the matter of finding an agent from outside to get into the vale. But I believe that if we can find such an agent, there may be a way to disable the barrier. If only for a moment so we could re-enter the vale."

"But we have so few men," Tharchelon said with despondence, a thousand thoughts competing for space in his head. "We would be at a serious disadvantage."

"We would have the advantage of surprise," said Rathenel. "Add to that the fact that Nelcherath is indecisive."

"Maybe in the dead of night?" Tharchelon mused.

"Indeed, Sire. And justice is on *our* side."

"Perhaps," said Tharchelon. "But the barrier?"

"The barrier derives its power from the magic that infuses the vale," Thockenar said. "If we can interrupt the source of magic to the barrier, it will fail."

"And how, pray tell, do we do that?" Tharchelon almost shouted. "You yourself just said that the magic infuses the entire vale!"

"This experience of exile has given me cause and new perspective to contemplate the nature of that magic, Highness," said Thockenar calmly. "Every one of our druids knows that the magic of the vale is strongest around the Bystle Tree. Indeed, inside the great trunk itself the magic is stronger still."

"So?" demanded Tharchelon. "Yes, yes. The great tree is the source of magic in the vale. Everyone knows that. Do you propose to set it ablaze to stop the magic? Chop it down perhaps?"

Thockenar actually cracked a smile. "Of course not, Highness. As I said, I have had occasion to reassess the nature of the magic in the vale. I wonder if the tree is not the source of magic, but is instead... a filter."

Tharchelon at once recognized the truth of it. "The Bystle Moss," he breathed.

"Indeed, Highness. I believe that the moss is the *true* source of magic, and the tree is but a conduit. Might there be a way to remove the moss from the tree without harming it?"

"No!" Tharchelon said emphatically. "No. It grows directly from the wood of the Bystle Tree. Besides, if it is indeed the true source of magic, why would the magic stop if the moss were removed?"

Thockenar looked thoughtful. "Yes, there is that, Highness."

"I think I may know the answer," Tharchelon said. "When I was a boy coming of age, my father tutored me on my duties in the moss garden. I never gave it much thought, but I asked him one day why so many Bystle Fruit-laden branches grew inward in the moss garden. He told me that he had once asked his father the very same question and was told that the moss loves light, especially the light of the Bystle Fruits. The tree helps tend to the needs of the moss and provides plenty of light to it by growing many fruits in the moss garden. The moss must have light all the time. The light gives life to the moss, and the moss gives life to the light."

Thockenar's normally stoic face registered genuine surprise. "So depriving the moss of light would stem the flow of magic into the vale?" He was like a little child in the wonderment of a new discovery. "And without a source of magic, the barrier would fail..."

Tharchelon considered the possibility. Perhaps it was true but he was unsure. The implications of being wrong cascaded through his mind. Even if the four interlopers still lived and agreed to help... even if they managed to make it to the moss garden and darken it... what if he and the old Druid were wrong? What if the barrier did not fall? A taste of moss would help him think.

"Is there no convincing Chetelar?" Tharchelon asked. "Is there no other partisan in the vale on whom we can rely?"

"If there is," Rathenel said, "he is unknown to us."

"Even if Chetelar could be convinced, Highness," Thockenar said, "would you trust him to complete the task? If he is caught, he will tell all he knows. Nelcherath will be warned and then be on guard. We have but one chance."

Tharchelon and his two advisors continued discussing and planning throughout the day and late into the night. Tharchelon decided in the end to tell them of the four outlanders who were coming, but not, of course, about the shadowy undead creature he had sent to hunt them.

They had no choice but to assume that depriving the moss of light would work. After all, if it did not, they would be no worse off than they were now. Success hinged on the four children.

They had set out before dawn to search for them. Worry was Tharchelon's constant companion until finally, in the early hours of the morning, a scout reported that four young humans had arrived at the top of the switchback trail at the rim of the chasm.

Elation! They had indeed survived Elija Abel. He gathered his advisors and some warriors and raced toward the edge of the gorge and the ancient ruined tower.

15th Day of Summer - 7:00 AM – Tower of Rovule – 15 Hours Until the Full Moon

Tharchelon watched the children race from the toppled obelisk to the edge of the gorge. The earthquake must have broken the dam. The implications of the dam breaking would have to wait as he had much more important matters at hand. Besides, the vale would not be in the path of the flood waters.

The children stood at the edge of the canyon, riveted to the destruction below. The thundering sound of the flood still filled the air.

A contingent of Tharchelon's soldiers arrived at that moment, putting a smile on his face. He nodded for them to follow him as he stepped out of his hiding place. As he approached the children, Tharchelon signaled his men to form up in a semi-circle around the group. The young humans did not hear them approach due to the rushing sound from the gorge. They turned in surprise when Tharchelon cleared his throat loudly.

The group looked like they had been to the Abyss and back; filthy mud-stained tunics, cuts, bruises and unkempt hair. The girl must be Brynn. The visitor in his dreams had repeated their names to him often. Ha! The visitor in his dreams: how long had it been since the accursed apparition had troubled him? It seemed an eternity.

The girl cast furtive glances to his warriors and the blue-eyed boy with a mop of brown hair. Cael?

The last two in the group of humans almost made him laugh out loud. There was an impossibly huge boy, nearly twice the height of a Rothkin. He had a sculpted head with a clean-shaven scalp. His chest was covered with angry scars. He looked a little pale despite having deeply tanned skin. Mallet? He stood near a scrawny boy whose bright eyes and white teeth stood as a sharp contrast to his dark skin and muddy, torn tunic. There was no doubt that this one was Needle.

Tharchelon marveled. They were so young! Were it not for the giant of a boy, Tharchelon would have thought it impossible that these kids could have escaped Letharchenel, much less Elija.

The brown-haired boy looked like he was trying to summon up his courage as he stepped forward. "My... my name is Cael Hotheway. We seek an audience with King Tharchelon."

CHAPTER THREE
Bargaining Chip

"You can motivate anyone if you can discover what motivates them..."

- General Yazak Thuune

15ᵗʰ Day of Summer - 7:00 AM – Tower of Rovule – 15 Hours to the Full Moon

"I... we... have been sent on an urgent errand and must speak with one called Tharchelon," said Cael. "Do you know him? Can you take us to him?"

None of the dozen or more Rothkin said anything in response. They were as short as the intruder Cael had seen lurking through his grandfather's cottage on the morning of the earthquake. Seeing these other Rothkin up close suddenly jarred his memory back to the intruder. Cael realized he hadn't given him much thought until now. It had been clear that morning that the little intruder had come to do murder, but Cael hadn't considered why... until now. He suddenly felt suspicious of these Rothkin.

Most were dressed in leather leggings and plain woolen tunics. Each carried a spear with a menacingly sharp flint blade. One of the warriors, with black hair and a chiseled face, wore black robes with a green crest over the breast. He stood next to the last man, who was clearly in command. He stood a full head taller than the rest, reaching maybe four and a half feet in height. He had chestnut hair and several days' growth of beard. His face, neck and arms were covered with scabs and bruises. His green eyes were intense, piercing.

"I am Tharchelon, King of the Bystle Vale," said the tall one finally, straightening up even more as he spoke. The king had a regal commanding presence, despite looking as if he had just gone to the hells and back.

"We have come for...," blurted Cael.

Tharchelon raised a finger with a stern look cutting him off. "Rathenel, take the others to the edge of the clearing and wait." He nodded to the one in black robes. As instructed, his soldiers marched off to the edge of the clearing, just out of earshot. Tharchelon stood quietly as he watched them go.

He looked like he had recently washed and put on fresh clothing that was a little ill-fitting, but the scabs and dark bruises indicated something dire had happened to him recently. He had dark circles under his eyes and Cael sensed that he was under intense stress despite his regal bearing. Cael felt like Tharchelon looked... horrible. After all, he and his companions had just virtually gone through the hells themselves. With the exception of a few days of respite on the river, they had been harried from the moment they first met in the Mausoleum and had to fight the wererat, Wheizer. The earthquake on the cliff, the sinkhole, the race to the docks, the mysterious invasion of their camp by an intruder, the journey through the swamp, the numerous fights with the awful creature that stalked them and finally the breaking of the dam and the death of Danilus. Boxxaway's letters implied that the journey to fetch the moss would be easy; perfunctory, in fact. Truth was, it had been a nightmare. Nothing had gone smoothly. He didn't even want to think about how they could get back to Demon's Bluff without Danilus and the boat.

"You have come for our sacred moss, I presume," said Tharchelon bluntly. His voice was subdued as if on cue with Cael's thoughts.

As bad as things had been up to now, the moment of Cael's worry was at hand. They had only one of the three tokens they were supposed to present to Tharchelon. How would the King react? He looked hard, uncompromising. Cael considered their options if this King refused to negotiate with them... none came to mind.

Mallet took a few steps forward and hunkered down, bringing himself more to an eye level with the Rothkin King. The move seemed very animal-like to Cael and he felt a sudden moment of panic. Among other things he didn't want to think about, was the whole issue of Mallet's lycanthropy... Needle took Mallet's cue and stepped forward also.

"Mallet?" asked Tharchelon, looking at the towering figure.

"How do you know his name?" Brynn asked, her brown eyes wide. She fidgeted with her tangled auburn hair.

"I've been expecting you. And from the looks of it, I was not the only one. Who, or what, is that creature?" He pointed over to where Elija had disappeared.

"You don't know him?" Cael asked.

Tharchelon shook his head.

"That thing has been stalking us for a week," Needle said. "He always seemed one step ahead of us."

Tharchelon looked confused. "Any idea why he was after you?"

"We were looking for tokens... to bring to you, in fact." said Cael. "Every place we went to look for them that creature was there first."

"Ah yes, the tokens," said Tharchelon. "Let's have them, then."

Cael desperately flailed about in his mind for how to answer. He could think of no option but the truth. "That creature destroyed all but one," said Cael finally, holding out his hand. The shiny black orb rolled back and forth in his palm.

Tharchelon studied him at length, a scowl slowly forming on this face. "How can I give you the moss if you cannot present all three tokens?"

"How did you know?" Needle asked.

Tharchelon looked irritated. "Know what?"

"Mallet's name," said Needle forcefully. "Brynn asked how you knew his name, and I think it's a good question." It occurred to Cael that he was watching something quite incongruous; a peasant making demands of a king.

"I have been dreaming about all of you for many months," Tharchelon replied, turning from Needle to address his response to Cael. "I know all your names."

"You dreamed our names?" Brynn asked, incredulous.

Cael looked over at her and instinctively knew what she was thinking. The fourth prophecy he had retrieved from the library and showed his companions on the boat ride north knew their names too. Surely Tharchelon's dreams were somehow frighteningly connected.

Tharchelon just shrugged. "Only one token?" he said as he rubbed the stubble on his chin. Cael could see the filth under his nails, and ugly yellowing bruises on his swollen fingers. "I think we have a problem."

Cael's heart sank but he forced himself to stand up straighter: "We need the moss."

"Why?" Tharchelon demanded.

Cael felt everything slipping away. They had come so far and fought so hard. This Rothkin wasn't about to simply turn the moss over to them. He could feel it. Not two weeks earlier he had been a carefree apprentice, studying magic under the tutelage of his grandfather. Had his decision to use the *Lorgnettes* to see his parents been the fateful decision that set him down this horrible path? Or would all this have happened anyway? He wanted to give up and go home... sleep in his own bed. But of course, that couldn't happen because his bed was at the bottom of that accursed sinkhole.

"My grandfather sent us. He told us to give you the tokens, and you would give us the moss."

"He was right," Tharchelon nodded. "But one token is not enough, I fear."

"What does it matter?" Needle shot back, a sudden intensity in his dark eyes. "Do the answers to who sent us and why influence your decision to give us the moss?"

"Who is this that speaks to me in such a manner?" Tharchelon's voice was austere, but Cael recognized anger when he saw it. What was Needle doing?

"I'm the kid in your dreams, that's who," Needle said forcefully.

"And?" demanded Tharchelon with a raised eyebrow.

"And why do you need tokens when your dreams told you we were coming for the moss?"

Tharchelon blinked.

"That's right!" exclaimed Brynn.

"Those tokens don't really matter to you, do they?" Needle demanded. "Who sent us and why doesn't matter either, does it?"

Mallet slowly stood. Cael flashed a quick glance to the warriors waiting by the edge of the clearing. There was no indication of movement or concern from them.

"You assume far too much," said Tharchelon after a pause. "My father instructed me, as he was in turn instructed by his father, and so on, back through the ages. We were to safeguard the sacred moss until such time as outlanders came bearing tokens from ancient times." A hint of a grin crossed his face. "As you do not possess all the correct tokens, you clearly are not they for whom we have been waiting."

"But you know we are!" Needle almost shouted. "You dreamed us!"

"And I should abandon the edict of my ancestors in favor of a dream?"

Cael noticed the warriors were stirring slightly.

"Wait just a son-of-Abyssin' minute," Mallet said suddenly. "Your ancestors knew we were coming? *For generations?*"

Tharchelon smiled a menacing, unpleasant smile. "That surprises you? I would have expected that were you truly those to whom I was to bequeath the moss, you would have known that such was the case."

"What?" asked a befuddled Mallet.

"He means yes, ya cheese-eater," said Needle sarcastically.

Mallet glowered.

"Your Highness," Cael offered. "It is true we lack two tokens, but is there no other option?" He wondered what his grandfather Boxxaway would say in this situation. Boxxaway had made it clear they were to obtain the moss to prevent the cult from getting it, at any cost. But how best to do that?

"C'mon, Cael!" shot Needle. "I told you this was fruitless when that creature destroyed the first token. We should just get the hells out of here and go back home."

"Your friend lacks faith," said Tharchelon.

Cael could see that Needle was trying to wrap his mind around the comment, assuming it was an insult. Cael however, immediately saw the underlying meaning of the statement. "So there *is* another option."

Tharchelon paused thoughtfully for several seconds. "As fate would have it, there may be a way we can help each other. Perhaps we each have a problem that only the other can solve. If you will help me solve my problem, I will solve yours."

"Does that mean you would give us the moss?" asked Needle.

"Indeed," said Tharchelon, addressing Cael.

Cael considered the option. "And what would be required of us?"

Tharchelon looked toward his warriors. "Recently there has been a coup in my kingdom," he said after a long pause. "Those warriors and I find ourselves exiled and unable to return to the vale."

"What?" cried Needle. "Cael, these inbred goat farmers don't even have the moss!"

Tharchelon flashed Needle a look that could melt glass. Needle didn't flinch.

"Is that true?" asked Brynn.

"It is the case, I'm afraid."

"Why don't you just take your warriors and sneak back in?" asked Mallet.

"Yes," said Tharchelon, stepping over to sit on a large stone. "About that. I should share some details with you."

Cael sat himself down on a stone of his own. Mallet re-hunkered.

"As King of the Vale, I have numerous advisers. Rathenel over there is among my most trusted." Tharchelon pointed over toward his warriors. "He wears the black robes." Needle repositioned himself for a better view of the warriors waiting at the edge of the clearing. Brynn did likewise.

"Another of my advisers, one called Nelcherath, was not so trustworthy," Tharchelon sighed. "I should start with the moss. The Bystle Moss is not plentiful, but it is the foundation of our culture. It is the source of all magic in the vale, and it gives life to the Bystle Tree, and light to its fruits."

"Bystle Tree?" asked Brynn.

"It is a huge tree that grows in the center of our vale. Its fruit glows and provides light and sustenance for my people.

My palace is inside the giant central trunk of the tree and there also grows the moss. The King began to salivate and wiped his mouth with a roughened palm. "This moss..." He paused, took a breath and continued. "This glorious, magical moss is the source of magic to the tree and our vale. Several weeks ago, I began to dream of your coming. I took Nelcherath into my confidence and told him that you would soon arrive and the foretold time when we would relinquish the moss was nigh."

"I knew it! The tokens don't matter at all!" Needle reiterated. "Do you realize we were chasing around fighting the Elija creature for nothing? We should have come straight here."

"You are the one who said we should go back," Brynn said with a stern look. Needle glared back.

"Nelcherath, it seems, found this news most unwelcome," the king continued as if Needle had said nothing. "Several days later, I was attacked as I slept. I was beaten, bound and exiled. Many others loyal to me received the same treatment. Nelcherath has exiled hundreds of us in the time since."

"We were still in Demon's Bluff, Cael," said Brynn. "He was dreaming of us and we hadn't even met each other yet!"

"So why don't you just sneak in and take back your kingdom?" asked Needle. "Or does he outnumber you that badly?"

"Nelcherath convinced our Druids to erect a magical barrier to keep us out. It encircles the vale completely, and none of us can pass back into the vale." Tharchelon continued to address Cael.

"I'm confused," said Cael. "Where do we figure in? We cannot pass the barrier either."

"We Rothkin cannot pass the barrier, but you four will be able to pass."

"How so?" asked Brynn.

"The barrier does not know you as it *knows* us. We are all infused by the magic of the vale, and you have never been exposed to it. As such, the barrier does not know you. You will be able to walk through it as if it were not there."

"And then what?" asked Mallet.

"You will need to eliminate the source of magic that powers the barrier. My warriors and I will rush in and surprise Nelcharath and the other traitors. We will retake power quickly."

"Eliminate the source of magic?" Cael asked.

"We will send you across the barrier later this morning. You should make your way to the large tree in the center of the vale, and find the sacred moss garden inside the trunk. The moss must be constantly bathed in light. If you darken the garden, the magic will cease to flow from the moss and the barrier will falter. We will be waiting at the edge of the barrier for that moment."

"Won't the tree be guarded?" Cael asked. "Wouldn't it be better to wait until dark?" The thought of tonight's full moon reminded Cael of Mallet's situation. He forced himself to put it out of his mind.

"Perhaps, but Nelcherath believes he is safe. They will not anticipate anything, especially an attack during the day."

"And how do we get into the tree?" Mallet asked.

Tharchelon adjusted his sitting position as he sat on the rock. "We have resources still inside the vale to help convey you to the tree. Rathenel will draw you a map so you will know the safest path to the moss garden once you are inside." Tharchelon pried a ring off one his fingers, and held it out to Cael. "This ring will open the portals inside the tree for you. If you are suitably stealthy, you should expect no trouble."

"So we get to the moss garden and darken it," Brynn said. "Then what?"

"Wait there for me. We will be victorious. Nelcherath and his guards will be completely surprised. Once we have secured the palace and captured the traitors, I will come for you."

"And you will give us the moss?" Needle asked, suspiciously.

"Yes," Tharchelon said, looking Needle in the eyes. "Not all of it. Our way of life depends on it, and we must keep just enough to re-grow our supply."

Cael was suddenly suspicious of this king. How could he know if he was telling the truth? A thought suddenly struck him. "About two weeks ago, as we were leaving Demon's Bluff, a Rothkin sneaked into my home. I hid from him and he did not find me, but I think he intended to kill me."

"Hey! I'd forgotten about that," Needle said. "What about that?"

Cael ignored Needle and carefully watched for Tharchelon's reaction. The king hesitated slightly, then said: "I am sure Nelcherath the traitor sent the assassin after you."

"How in the hells would he know to do that?" Needle demanded.

"As I said before, I told him of my dreams," Tharchelon said calmly. "He knew your names and I'm sure he acted preemptively to defend the moss and our way of life. Perhaps he sent that creature after you as well."

The answer sounded reasonable to Cael. Perhaps this Tharchelon was being truthful. Cael noticed Needle was also watching Tharchelon closely.

"How much moss will we get?" Brynn asked.

Tharchelon considered the question. "I'll give you all of it, save a little to re-establish a crop."

"But how much is that?" Brynn pressed.

"It doesn't weigh much. Many ounces at least, I would think," said the King.

"You know what I think?" said Needle slowly. "I think this son of Abyss is a liar, Cael. I don't trust this spuddy little runt one bit."

Tharchelon was taken aback, and it took several seconds for Needle's words to fully register. Cael could see the fury building on the king's countenance. In a flash, Cael knew of a certainty that Needle was right in his assessment. *Tharchelon was lying!*

The king whistled loudly as he stood up. His warriors stirred and started toward them. Cael had no idea how to react to this situation. It was unfolding far too fast and no options were evident. Mallet was hesitating as well and Brynn looked utterly confused.

With lightning speed, Tharchelon surged forward and jammed his fist into Cael's midsection. The blow was delivered with astounding force, given the small stature of the Rothkin King. Cael felt a sense of overwhelming panic as his wind left him and he doubled over.

"Subdue them!" Tharchelon shouted as he spun backward and kicked Needle in the stomach with his heel. Tharchelon's warriors had already flashed into action before their king even gave the command. Needle also doubled over as he gulped for air. "Runt, am I?" Tharchelon howled.

Through his pain, Cael could see the scrambling boots of the Rothkin warriors as they closed in. Tharchelon jumped to one side as the blade of Mallet's glaive came down and sunk itself into the sod. Cael felt a blinding pain and a jarring flash of brightness in his eyes. It took him a second to realize that Tharchelon had taken the opportunity to kick him full force in the side of the head as he sidestepped Mallet's attack.

Tharchelon whirled like a dune dervish and slipped between Mallet's legs, taking the opportunity to punch him in the crotch as he did so. Mallet's eyes bulged as he doubled over.

Tharchelon whipped a knife from his boot and spun over to Needle, holding it to his neck. The flint blade glinted in the morning sun as a swarm of Rothkin warriors overwhelmed Mallet. Brynn was similarly swarmed over, but only after she slashed more than one Rothkin with her knife.

Cael finally was able to suck in a breath of air, only to find himself being hog tied with straps of leather. His three companions were in the same sorry state.

In short order, they found themselves being frog marched eastward along a foot path at spear point by Tharchelon's brethren.

"What now?" Cael called ahead to Tharchelon.

The king slowed his pace, allowing Cael to catch up to him. "We proceed with the plan," Tharchelon said with a grin. "But with one minor change."

"You sent the assassin," Cael said.

"Rathenel!" Tharchelon called to the front of the column. "Take three warriors with you and escort the mouthy one back to our camp. Keep him under armed guard. Gather everyone who can fight and meet me at the goat head rock. I'll take the rest of the warriors and escort these three to the barrier. Make haste and meet me there no later than two hours from now."

Rathenel jerked Needle out of the line, and indicated the three closest warriors to accompany him. They trudged off through the trees to the north east. Needle looked back over his shoulder, genuine fear in his eyes. Cael felt utterly helpless.

"You three will enter the vale, darken the moss garden and wait patiently there for me to arrive, just as we discussed. You aren't to touch the moss."

"What if we just decide to warn everyone once we get in?" Mallet asked. Cael already knew the answer before Tharchelon confirmed it.

"You will do as I tell you," smiled Tharchelon cruelly. "Or your friend will suffer the long and slow death he deserves."

CHAPTER FOUR
Remembrance

"Time it seems, is as flexible as the weather itself. The exception to this, as everyone knows, is the Astral. On that plane, time is a constant that cannot be bent except by the rare and fabled astral storms."

- Horlocher Munro, Stormsage of Taglyon

15th Day of Summer - 10:00 AM – The Barrier – 12 Hours Until the Full Moon

"We are at the barrier," a Rothkin guard called back.

"I don't see anything," said Brynn, craning her neck to peer ahead through the dense forest.

Cael couldn't see anything either… but he could *feel* something. They had been marched along the foot path for almost three hours before Tharchelon led them off the path into a thickly forested area. After another fifteen minutes or so of trudging through the humid forest, they arrived. It was about two hours before noon.

Armed Rothkin warriors, with King Tharchelon himself, were arrayed around them. On Tharchelon's order, the captives' bindings were removed. Cael rubbed his aching wrists. The still-healing wound on his palm ached fiercely. Sunlight hid behind a canopy of leaves and branches while a chorus of birds sang discordant songs. The smell of the pungent earth permeated everything, as if the whole forest was rotting.

There was something strange going on with the *Arcanus Navitas*. It was here… it was strong… but it was inaccessible. He felt like he was chasing fireflies when his mind reached out to grab it.

Mallet stepped forward, squinting and rubbing his own wrists. "That's because there's nothing there."

"Show them," Tharchelon said abruptly.

One of the little warriors stepped up and pressed both hands against an invisible barrier, leaning far forward. There was little doubt that his hands were pressed against something unseen that held him up.

"Whoa," Mallet said has he started walking toward the barrier. Several guards turned their spears on him, stopping him short.

"What word from Chetelar?" Tharchelon asked. As if on cue, an old Rothkin with bushy eyebrows limped out of the underbrush about thirty yards on the other side of the barrier. He was dressed in a shabby tunic and leggings that were rent in places. He stopped about ten yards short of the barrier, looking around furtively. "M-m-m'Lord," he stuttered.

Tharchelon ignored the forlorn character and turned his attention to Cael, handing him a rolled parchment. "Do you still have the ring I gave you?"

Cael nodded, unrolling the scroll. It contained a simple and clear map.

"It marks the safest path through the interior trunk of the Bystle Tree to the moss garden," Tharchelon continued. "Chetelar will guide you through the forested areas of the vale to keep you unseen. He will show you to a secret entrance among exposed roots of the tree. The door will open for you if you wear that ring."

"What will happen to Needle?" Brynn demanded.

Tharchelon cracked a brief smile. "That, my dear, depends entirely upon you. You will enter the moss garden and darken it. You will wait there for me, touching nothing. If you fail in any aspect of that, I will see to it that your friend's short life is filled with agony. I'll not forget to remind him constantly of your betrayal to him."

Cael frowned. Tharchelon's threats were growing increasingly cruel.

"You realize," said Mallet, "you need us as much as we need

you. And your threats are completely unnecessary and asinine. If you had asked nicely, we would have gladly helped you, but instead you resort to manipulation and coercion."

Cael blinked. Had Mallet ever said that many words in one sentence?

Tharchelon just smiled. "Your perceptions about everything are incorrect." He nodded to one of his warriors, who pushed Cael forward.

Cael walked slowly, his hand held out, feeling for the barrier. He suddenly remembered a childhood game, being blindfolded and pawing the air carefully to find and strike a suspended bag filled with treats. How old had he been? Five? Six?

He felt a warm charge in the air. He could feel the *Arcanus Navitas* suddenly thin out to almost nothing as he moved forward. He stopped.

"Make haste," Tharchelon commanded. "The barrier does not know you and will not stop you. Step forward."

Cael took several more steps, his hand held out. He was now in a place where the *Arcanus Navitas* was utterly empty. This was a weird sensation for him. Since he was a young boy, when his grandfather had painstakingly taught him how to sense the *Arcanus Navitas* on their regular desert walks, it had always been present: sometimes plentifully and sometimes more sparsely. Sometimes there were eddies and currents, but it was never, *ever*, just absent.

He took another step and felt something. It was neither cool nor warm, but it was solid. When he pushed his hand against it, he found it was completely smooth and as unforgiving as a brick wall.

He looked back, and Tharchelon had a very puzzled look on his face. The other Rothkin regarded him suspiciously. "Have you been in the vale before?" King Tharchelon demanded. Cael shook his head and tried again.

He pushed against the invisible barrier again and still it stopped him short.

Tharchelon stepped forward, his face morphing into fury. Cael pushed again at the unyielding, invisible wall and this time it yielded a little. It felt leathery and pliant. He pressed forward a little more and then it suddenly gave way and absorbed him. He passed through it and tumbled forward, almost losing his balance. Chetelar limped over to steady him.

Cael instantly felt something intensely strange with the *Arcanus Navitas*... or what should have been the *Arcanus Navitas*. In its place was some imposter. What should have been the familiar embrace of the flowing magic was something foreign... alien. It seemed to Cael like taking a bite of something he expected to be sweet and delicious, only to find a mouthful of salty bitterness. The flow pattern of this new magical energy was unfamiliar, too. It swirled and behaved in unnatural ways. He experimented with taking in a small amount but found he could not hold on to it.

Cael turned around and looked back at Tharchelon. The malicious little king stared at him with barely disguised hatred as he strode forward to test the integrity of the barrier himself. Sure enough, it did not yield for him. He pressed his full weight against it, a confused look on his face.

With a nod of his head, the warriors pushed first Brynn, then Mallet forward and each in turn crossed through the barrier. As happened with Cael, the barrier at first stopped them, but then allowed them to push through.

"We will keep our part of the bargain and darken the moss chamber," Cael said. Did the king's lip twitch at the mention of the moss? "And lower the barrier," he continued. "And you will keep your part of the bargain and give us the moss and Needle."

The king *had* twitched. *He's got no intention of freeing us, and there is no way in hells he's giving us the moss.*

Cael watched Mallet chuckle, an evil gleam in his eye as he stared down the king. Cael felt a deep moment of satisfaction when he saw Tharchelon blanch and turn away.

15ᵗʰ Day of Summer - 3:00 PM – The Bystle Tree – 7 Hours to the Full Moon

"Did you hear something?" Mallet hissed. Chetelar led them limping through the most heavily wooded areas inside the vale to avoid being spotted. There was no indication they were anywhere near a populated area until they had crossed an irrigation ditch that afforded them a quick glimpse of a pasture occupied by several dozen sheep.

"Besides the birds?" Cael whispered back. Walking through the forest was eerily similar to dodging down the tight constricted alleys of Demon's Bluff.

"No, really," Mallet said, stopping.

"Maybe it's Chetelar," Brynn said, wiping sweat from her forehead with the back of her hand.

"No, it's coming from behind us," Mallet insisted. Cael listened for a moment but could not hear anything but birds.

"I can't believe Needle is not here," said Cael. He never thought he'd miss the Agrabi boy, but he did. If he hadn't been captured, there would be so many options to get out of their mess. But as long as he was being held captive, there wasn't much they could do but simply comply with Tharchelon's wishes, and hope some option presented itself. Every time Cael tried to game out their choices in his mind, it always ended in Needle's horrible death. It seemed that Tharchelon held Needle as the ultimate trump card. Unless they simply left Needle to his fate and hoped for the best... but something would not let Cael consider abandoning Needle.

Chetelar limped out from some brush up ahead. "We are very near the Bystle Tree now," he whimpered as he scanned the area with a worried look on his face. They had been slithering around, following him for nearly five hours. Sometimes they stayed put in the underbrush until it was okay to proceed. Other times, they took circuitous routes to stay in the overgrown areas as much as possible. Chetelar seemed increasingly exhausted and terrified with each passing hour.

They followed him to the edge of a large clearing. Cael peered out at the largest tree he had ever seen. Many times larger, in fact, than the tree in the swamp that led down to the Cult's hidden temple. Brynn bumped into him and he heard her suck in her breath at the sight.

The massive trunk must have been a full forty yards in diameter. It reached hundreds of feet into the sky. Huge round leaves hung from its branches, along with thousands of yellow fruits. Though the sun was high in the sky, by the shade of the massive tree, Cael could see that each fruit emitted a yellow light. The sight was altogether ethereal. The flowing alien magic here had grown stronger, and it flowed at Cael directly from the tree. He had been practicing taking some in, and found that with extreme concentration he could do it.

"Holy demon mother!" Mallet whispered, looking at the amazing sight.

They could see a few guards walking catwalks high in the branches of the tree. Chetelar indicated through pointing and hand gestures that they should stay quiet and follow him quickly. He pointed to a tangle of gigantic roots that breached the ground around the tree close to where they were hidden at the edge of the clearing. The roots wrapped around the back side of the tree. Cael saw that if they could cross the fifteen-foot gap to the tangle of roots unseen, they could move about without drawing attention.

Chetelar, though timid and afraid, hobbled quickly across the gap, timing his crossing perfectly. By following his well-timed signals, they were able to cross safely, one at a time.

"What in the name of the hells?" Mallet whispered, coming to a complete stop as they followed their Rothkin guide through the maze of huge roots.

Thousands of tiny faces peered out at them from an ivy covered section of roots. Mallet crept over the mossy ground to the ivy wall, parted the foliage and felt one of the faces. "Wood carvings..." he whispered.

"They are memorials to our dead," Chetelar said in the quietest of voices. "The wall is a remembrance of our ancestors. Family members carve the faces of their deceased loved ones here."

"Where is the entrance?" Cael asked.

"We are close," the bushy-browed Rothkin said, looking around furtively. "It is just up ahead."

The air was warm. An occasional beam of sunlight managed to reach down through the leaves and tangle of roots. Dust and pollen could be seen riding the slow air currents in the light. Bird songs smoothed to a gentle hum that seemed to match the rhythm of their footfalls over the green, mossy ground.

"You folk really are quite big," Chetelar whispered, looking up at Mallet. "I never seen your like before."

They wound a few more steps through the labyrinthine roots until they came between two exceptionally large sections of root that formed a 'V' close to the trunk. It seemed to provide less cover and Cael felt vulnerable as they came to the trunk at the bottom of the 'V'.

As if on cue with his worry, a shadow passed over them.

"Merciful hells!" Chetelar breathed, a panicked look on his face.

A wooden flying machine descended from the trees like a raptor. It looked like a buckboard wagon with wings. A Rothkin in the front piloted the magical glider while a second Rothkin sat strapped onto a raised platform behind the pilot. He manned a bizarre-looking ballista. One of the glowing bystle fruits, a large one, was impaled upon a wooden spike that seemed to grow from the rear of the flyer.

Cael looked around. The flying contraption must have been on some sort of patrol and spotted them. His mind raced for a solution to their predicament, but they really had nowhere to run.

The flyer swooped down and came to light on the ground behind them in one smooth motion. The Rothkin manning the ballista aimed the menacing weapon toward them.

Cael cursed their luck. They had carefully woven their way through the vale for hours on end without being spotted, only to be caught at the last possible moment.

"Here!" Chetelar hissed, jerking on Cael's tunic, and pointing to a section of exposed root. "The hidden door is here."

The gunner drew a bead and fired. A bolt of lightning sizzled from the end of the weapon and struck the ground at their feet, sending a spray of moist earth and smoking green moss in all directions.

Chetelar screamed and wound himself up to flee but there was nowhere for him to go. Cael watched the panicked Rothkin lose his composure entirely, finally charging toward the grounded craft, seeking to run around it in his hobbling gait.

The gunner unleashed another thunderbolt from his weapon and Chetelar's head exploded in a spray of red mist. The rest of him tumbled to the ground in a twitching heap.

CHAPTER FIVE
Old Friends
"Fate will find a way to have its purposes fulfilled."

- Blodwynn Vallant

15th Day of Summer – 7:30 AM – The Tower of Rovule – Less than 15 hours to the Full Moon

Needle looked back over his shoulder at Cael, Mallet and Brynn as they continued marching along the trail. They looked desperately scared. One of his captors poked him with the butt of a glinting spear and indicated with a glance that he should keep his eyes front and pay attention to marching. The leather straps that bound his hands behind his back were incredibly tight. He was pretty sure he could slip them, but it would take time and effort. Of course, he could make no progress while he was being watched by these Rothkin.

"Where are we going?" he asked the black-robed Rathenel, who marched directly in front of him.

This was the second time in as many weeks that he had been trussed up and marched off to captivity. In the first case, he could at least take comfort in the fact that Wheizer would keep him alive for profit at the slave markets of Balankov. With these Rothkin, there was no such assurance. In fact, as he thought it through, it was clear that Cael had no leverage at all over this Rothkin King. That he was a liar was evident to Needle, and once he got whatever it was that he needed from Cael, Mallet and Brynn, he would have no need for any of them. Would he simply let them go? Doubtful.

The realization spurred him at least to try *something*. He cautiously tested the strength and tightness of his bonds again. It wasn't long before the Rothkin behind him noticed and jabbed him in the back of the head with the butt of a spear. To add insult to injury, the Rothkin pulled out his water skin and poured water over Needles wrists. Rope? *Easy.* Leather tongs? *Difficult.* Wet leather? *Nearly impossible.*

They marched along through dense forest. The trees, underbrush and smells were all completely new to him, but he had no heart to pay much notice. That flood must certainly have killed Danilus and Dheke. The roar of the broken dam had subsided with distance. What would become of Demon's Bluff when the flood waters arrived there? No doubt the people of the Lower Steppe would suffer the most, and none more than his people living in the Kuma. As usual, the nobles on the Middle Steppe would be spared. The injustice of it all was overwhelming.

If there was any bright spot in his current situation, he would at least be spared a terrifying *death-by-wererat* when Mallet shifted at the full moon tonight. Cael and Brynn were surely goners, but they were all likely goners anyway. Maybe Mallet would be able to take a few dozen of these little goat molesters out in the process.

After a couple of hours of marching, they entered a large encampment. Needle estimated there were a several hundred of the little Rothkin, including many women and children. They huddled around their morning cook fires in front of poorly constructed pine-bough lean-tos. *A refugee camp!* He was paraded through the camp toward a large wigwam structure near the center. Every Rothkin they passed stared at him as if they had never seen such a sight. Was it his dark skin, or the fact that he towered over them? Probably both, he decided.

They threw him into the wigwam and promptly tied him to one of the four log support pillars. They sat him with his back to the pillar and re-tied his hands behind it. They bound his feet and gave his leather straps another good soaking. There would be no escape, at least not anytime soon.

Needle looked around. There was a smoldering fire and a few very small chairs made of branches tied together with leather straps. The only light came from a smoke hole in the ceiling, and through gaps in the branches and animal skins that covered the structure. There was nothing he could use here to free himself.

He examined the gaps where the walls met the floor around the structure. With his hands free he'd probably be able to loosen it up, or dig under and slip out without much difficulty.

No sooner did he have the thought than the edge of the gap started to move. Some little creature stuck its nose in the gap, then started to squeeze through. A rat? And it was a big one, too; as long as Needle's forearm and maybe a little thicker. Certainly bigger than any rat he had ever seen in the Kuma... and there were some big rats in the Kuma.

The worm-tailed creature wriggled itself all the way in and sniffed around its immediate vicinity. It stayed where it was for about two minutes, almost as if it were letting its eyes grow accustomed to the lower light level. It occasionally rose up on its haunches, and sniffed at the air. It seemed to Needle very peculiar behavior for an animal.

The rodent apparently got its bearings and began to saunter directly over to him. Needle had often heard horror stories about vagrants in Demon's Bluff who had their toes nibbled off by gutter rats as they slept.

Needle froze.

What in the holy hells?

Needle felt as if his blood were draining away. The rat before him started to grow in size. It began slowly at first, then accelerated as it ballooned to many times its original size. Panic seized Needle. He could not move... he could not speak. Mallet must have ratted out early and killed everyone he was with! In the lycanthropic grip of blood lust fever, he must have decided to hunt down a familiar target to kill... his old friend, Needle!

The rat creature indeed began to shape shift, taking on a more human form. Arms and legs lengthened, fingers extended, head and neck rounded out, fur thinned. The half-rat, half-man creature before him was grotesque. Needle shut his eyes tight, waiting for the inevitable bite that he knew was only moments away.

Only... the bite did not come. After what seemed like an eternity, Needle opened one eye. The horror was more awful even than he could have expected.

There, smiling, before him on one knee, stark naked, was

none other than *Wheizer Rhelbog.*

"You know, Needle," Wheizer said in a low voice, "seems like every time we meet, you have managed to get yourself captured."

Needle's brain could not react. He just sat there dumbstruck. This was impossible. Wheizer was dead. He had plunged the silver dagger into his chest himself. He had to be dead.

"Well, it's lucky for you, your old friend Wheizer is here to save you." Wheizer bounded stealthily over to where he had entered. He reached under the wall of the wigwam and pulled in his clothes and rapier. "You'd think these little Rothkin would notice a rat dragging a bundle of clothes. But the whole damn camp is in an uproar. Every male in the place is getting ready to march off to war."

Needle sat frozen, but indeed there was quite a clamor going on outside. He could hear orders being barked above the general din.

"Hey. Look what I stole," Wheizer said after he quickly dressed. He held up Needle's silver dagger. "Apparently these little bastards don't trust you with this." Wheizer flipped the blade over in the air before him and caught it by the handle as he started walking back toward Needle. "This ain't the same blade as you jabbed in my chest at the docks, is it, Needle?"

This was it. His moment had come. His father was gone, and now his mother was also dead. Perhaps it was fitting that the same creature that killed her would also kill him with the very blade she had given him. Needle's father had always counseled him not to fear death, and to welcome it when the time came. Thus, Needle always assumed he'd be at peace when the moment of his death came. But it wasn't that way at all. He was so young, and there were so many things he wanted to do in his life. He still needed to find his father... he suddenly realized he'd never see him again. Maybe if his father had indeed died, he'd be seeing him again shortly in the afterlife. It was no comforting thought. He did not want to die.

To his amazement, Wheizer used the blade to cut first the leathers that tied his legs, then slid behind him and cut his hands free. "We don't have much time if we are going to sneak out of here," Wheizer said, his voice still low. "The chaos out there ain't gonna last forever."

"You're... not going to kill me?" Needle finally croaked.

"Kill you? Tsk, tsk, tsk," Wheizer flashed a wicked grin. "Don't you know I always keep my promises? You still have value to me."

"You came all this way just so you could sell me as a slave?" Needle asked, bewildered.

"You are full of yourself, aint' you, boy? You're gonna help me save Mallet, and maybe Brynn. But that depends on my mood when the time comes. If we get lucky, we might just get in there and get me some of that moss everyone keeps jabberin' about."

"How do you know about the moss?" Needle blinked.

"You are hurting my feelings, Needle. I got ears, after all. And in case you hadn't noticed, I'm pretty damn sneaky. And clever, if I don't say so myself."

"It was you at the camp!" Needle breathed. "How close did Danilus come to catching you?"

"Nice! Intelligent slaves are worth so much more than dumb ones."

"Why would you possibly want the moss?" Needle asked. This entire conversation seemed surreal.

"Cause everyone else does, you dumb bastard."

"You don't even know what it's for!"

"Does it matter? How do you think business works kid? You get stuff everyone wants and then you sell it to the highest bidder." Wheizer pulled Needle to his feet and shoved him toward the back of the wigwam. "Sides, from what little I heard, seems like your wizard friend don't know what it's good for neither."

Wheizer dropped to one knee, jabbing Needle's dagger through the hide that made the back wall and peered through the hole. "Now's the time, kid," he said as he extended the slit all the way down to the floor. He sheathed the dagger and drew his rapier. "I don't see anyone. They must be sendin' their battalion off."

The light outside seemed incredibly bright as they stepped out. Needle was worried that they'd be spotted, but there wasn't a soul around, just as Wheizer had said. There was plenty of commotion coming from the eastern end of the camp; clanking noises and shouted orders.

In no time, they had slunk past half a dozen lean-tos and into the forest. Needle considered just making a break for it and trying to escape, but Wheizer had his father's silver dagger. Besides, it wasn't likely he could outrun the wererat anyway.

Before long they came to a stream. "This flows downstream from the Vale," Wheizer said. "We follow this and we'll be there in maybe half an hour."

"How do you know?" Needle asked.

"You think I just sit on my ass all day, don't you, boy?" Wheizer snarled. "When I do a job, I do it right. I had that vale already scouted out top to bottom long before you and your buddies even got up here. Nobody pays attention to rats, Needle."

"What job?"

"Are all Agrabi as nosy and stupid as you?" Wheizer shook his head in disbelief. "I got to bring Mallet back to his father."

"The full moon," Needle breathed.

Wheizer just laughed. "With all those questions you got, have you asked yourself why I'm not worried about you runnin' on me?"

"Cause you have the dagger my mother gave me."

Wheizer laughed again. Needle could feel the blood surging into his face.

"You killed my mother!" he whispered.

"I never touched her!" Wheizer grinned. "Besides, with the dam busted, I'm thinking she would have had a good drowning to look forward to. If I did kill her, I did her and you a favor."

Rage overwhelmed Needle. He charged at Wheizer and managed to punch him in the face before the stunned wererat could even react.

"You little Agrabi bastard!" Wheizer spat, wiping blood that ran in a trickle from his nose. Wheizer picked him up and hurled him against a tree. Needle's vision went black. His senses cleared when Wheizer bent over him. Something sticky was running down the back of his neck.

Wheizer punched him in the stomach, knocking the wind out of him again. He turned sideways and crawled frantically away, but got a brutal kick in the ribs.

A hand grabbed his hair again and shoved his face deep into the loamy earth. Wet dirt from the stream bank filled his mouth, nose and eyes. "You soulless Agrabi runt," Wheizer breathed in his ear.

He flipped Needle over onto his back and punched him in the face. Needle had been in a few fights before. Growing up in the Kuma was tough, but he had never been hit with such force; Wheizer's strength was inhuman.

"You little whelp," Wheizer hissed, drawing Needle's dagger. "I should slice open your belly and string you up by your own intestines. I should cut your eyes out with this blade you stabbed me with."

Needle stayed conscious, struggling for air. His face was swelling. Blood spilled from his nose and from what must be a gash where the back of his head impacted the tree. The beating Wheizer had given him a few weeks earlier had been nothing compared to what he had just gotten.

Needle laughed, gurgling blood. There wasn't anything funny about what was happening, but there it was. He laughed.

Wheizer grunted, "You're one of a kind," and reached down and grabbed Needle by the arm and jerked him to his feet. "Killing you would be too easy. You're coming with me and you're gonna watch me welcome Mallet into the domain of lycanthropy. Maybe I'll let him murder his sister before I let him kill you."

Needle stopped laughing.

Wheizer pushed him along and somehow Needle managed to stay upright. At this moment, there was absolutely nothing he could do. Wheizer had him, and that was that. But if he kept moving, breathing, getting his strength back… he needed to stay alert.

Wheizer's rage was spent, but the ease of his victory would hopefully lower his guard.

Suddenly, Needle felt a strange sensation in his body as Wheizer pushed him along. He bumped into something that wasn't there. Wheizer gave him another shove forward and it felt like he was being enveloped by something that held him in some sort of invisible embrace, then spat him out on the other side. It must be the barrier the Rothkin King spoke of.

He turned to watch Wheizer walk straight into the unseen barrier. It flattened his face for a moment. Wheizer cursed and fell right on his ass. Blood poured from his nose. He looked utterly baffled.

Wheizer stepped forward again (a bit more carefully, however), pressed both hands against the invisible barrier and gave it a mighty shove. If he had been trying to move a mountain it would have had the same result. He backed up and rammed the unseen wall with his shoulder, but it didn't give an inch.

There might just be a little justice in this wretched world after all...

"What unholy whoredom is this?" Wheizer demanded.

Needle blinked, wobbled and stood still, watching Wheizer. "The barrier," said Needle. "You've already been in the vale, you dumb rat bastard."

Wheizer didn't answer, but the expression on his face said it all. One minute, he had Needle completely where he wanted him, and the next Needle was absolutely free.

Needle resisted the urge to taunt and provoke. Instead, he did something far better. With Wheizer so dumbfoundedly distracted, he reached across the barrier and snatched his dagger from Wheizer's belt. To his amazement, it worked.

Needle laughed out loud. A deep gratitude filled him, something he wasn't necessarily equipped to handle. Tears filled his eyes. This was perfect. As bad as his life had been since his father had disappeared, and even worse in the past few weeks, this moment was perfect.

He turned and followed the stream through the woods. Cael, Brynn and Mallet were in here somewhere.

Wheizer stood seething helplessly at the barrier.

CHAPTER SIX
Backup Plan

"Every problem has a solution."

- Wheizer Rhelbog

15th Day of Summer - 2:00 PM – The Barrier – 8 Hours Until the Full Moon

Wheizer watched the little Agrabi son of a whore disappear into the chaparral with a final smirk over his shoulder.

Needle had escaped... again.

Wheizer had to restrain himself from reaching out and smashing his fingers on the barrier... again.

It was sheer dumb luck. All that talk about a barrier preventing return to the vale had seemed like some elaborate lie from the little trampy Rothkin King. Apparently there was more to it than he had assumed.

He felt along the perfectly smooth surface of the invisible barrier. He had seen plenty of magic done in his day, but he had never seen anything like this. Imagine how useful something like this would be! He remembered the Rothkin king saying that the moss was the power source for the vale. Did that mean it also powered this barrier? All the more reason to steal it.

He grinned. He was starting to think that moss was going to be even more valuable than he had hoped.

The problem, of course, was that he was on the wrong side of the barrier. How to get the moss? And then there was the issue of Mallet. Looking at the sun, he gauged it was an hour or two after noon; eight or nine hours to dark and *his* son's first glorious transformation.

And yet... if Mallet ratted out without him there to manage him, he'd surely kill everyone around him. Wheizer didn't care at all about the Cael kid, but he would hate to see Needle get off so easily. Losing Brynn would actually be a good riddance as far as Wheizer was concerned, and Dagorn would get over it...eventually. But Mallet would be inconsolable and therefore worthless... for months... even *years*. And wouldn't Wheizer know? The horrible things he had done when he first turned had haunted him for years. He pushed the memories from his mind. Even now, over twenty years later, the recollection was still far too painful.

Then there was also the very real possibility that Mallet would kill himself out of anguish. He'd wouldn't be the first new wererat to take that path.

Wheizer's only hope, then, was for the four kids to succeed in their mission and secure the moss, bringing down the barrier.

How likely was that?

In a way, allowing Needle to go and help them might actually improve their chances. The little bastard had proved more resourceful than Wheizer ever would have guessed.

So? Nothing to do but wait. And that led him to consider the improbable events that had brought him to this unlikely place...

2nd Day of Summer – 7:00 AM – Dagorn's Estate – 1 Day After the Earthquake

Wheizer's head hurt. No. *Everything hurt.*

He slowly became aware that ropes were tied to his wrists and ankles. He could feel a dull pain through the numbness of his feet and hands. His joints ached mercilessly. He flexed his muscles against the tension of the ropes, but they were unforgiving.

He opened his eyes to a candle-lit chamber. He recognized

it immediately; it was the chamber behind Dagorn's collection room. This is where he kept the best of his collection, including a torture rack recovered from a Cult of Yex dungeon and painstakingly restored. It didn't take long to realize it was that rack upon which he was being stretched.

He had himself recommended this to Dagorn, to stretch him out so his bones could be re-broken thus allowing them to knit back in their proper positions. He must have blacked out from the pain. He refocused on the pain he felt now. Yes, it was just joint pain from the stretching of the rack itself. His bones were hopefully set straight and healed. He could move his head just enough to know he was alone. Why would Dagorn leave him?

No sooner had he formed that thought than Dagorn entered the chamber and stood over him, setting down his ever present wine goblet. Dagorn smiled at him.

"That was kind of fun," Dagorn said as he released the catch on the rack. Wheizer felt the ropes go slack and the pain in his joints immediately eased.

"Glad I could entertain," Wheizer rasped as he slipped his wrists free. "How long was I unconscious?"

"If you just woke up, then about half an hour," Dagorn said as he loosened the nooses around Wheizer's ankles. "I had to pull some strings but I arranged a transport for you."

"Transport?" Wheizer asked, as he rubbed the blood back into his hands and feet.

"Out in the courtyard," Dagorn said, leading Wheizer out. "The wreckage out there in town is unbelievable. We got lucky."

Wheizer hobbled along, still moving gingerly. They turned the corner into the courtyard, and before them was a Gryphon. A majestic creature, half-mountain lion and half-vulture, its black feathers gave way to gray fur. Its piercing bird eyes focused on them as they approached. It stood nearly five feet high at the shoulder and was probably twelve feet long, beak to tail. Its massive wings were folded along its sides, but Wheizer estimated the wingspan would be over twenty feet. Its beak was pierced with a large iron ring clamped through. Reins tied to the steel ring allowed a rider to control the mount. The reins were tied around the low branch of one of the mesquite trees that grew around the courtyard. The creature sharpened its claws absently on the trunks of the tree. A finely-crafted saddle rode high on its back, the saddle horn right between the beast's massive wings.

"Nice," Wheizer said, filled with a moment of awe. "He got a name?"

"Valsipherus," said Dagorn. "Had to cash in a favor. Can you find them before... you know?"

"I got two weeks." Wheizer said, waving his hand in a 'no problem' gesture. "Should be more than enough time."

"What do you think they are up to?"

"Ah.... that's the question. I think I'll take it slow and see if I can't listen in and find out what's going on. That thing in the mausoleum with Elowynn has got me spooked."

"You're certain she didn't tell them anything?" Dagorn asked.

"We been through this," said Wheizer. "I'm certain. Brynn didn't learn a thing. But the question is, what have they learned on their own? What are they up to?"

"Mallet got a peek before he was ready," said Dagorn. "You think that set them all off?"

"No," said Wheizer, stroking the beak of the magnificent beast. "It's something to do with Brynn and Elowynn, and for all we know, Kemano and Needle. I'll find out."

3rd Day of Summer - The Demon River - 12 Days to the Full Moon

From his high vantage atop Valsipherus, it didn't take long for Wheizer to locate the river boat. There was very little river traffic north of Demon's Bluff, and with the sullen storm clouds, it wasn't hard to blend into the sky and stay unseen.

He gave them plenty of distance and only risked flying in closer during the late evening hours. It was entirely unlikely that he'd be able to get close enough to hear anything, and getting on that boat was also probably out of the question. In fat form, he might pull it off, but to what purpose? And the benefit certainly didn't outweigh the risk. No. He'd have to wait until the right opportunity presented itself. Eventually, they would get sick of the close quarters on that boat.

7ᵗʰ Day of Summer - 7:00 PM – Eastern Shore of the Demon River – 8 Days to the Full Moon

It wasn't too many days before he had his opportunity to get near them. Near sunset, they beached the boat on the eastern riverbank, and started to make camp about a hundred yards from the river. It looked like they were intending to stay the night. The wizard boy and the red-headed stranger headed off to a mesquite thicket. Wheizer watched from a great distance, keeping himself between the sun and his prey.

He'd have to move fast. He circled around to the south and made a very low approach astride Valsipherus. Flying northward just a few feet above the river, he estimated he would remain unseen. About a quarter mile south of the beached boat, he alighted and secured Valsipherus. He pulled two thick, long strips of partially dried meat from one of the saddle bags and tossed them in the sand at the great beast's feet. The Gryphon snatched one of the meat strips in its beak and held down the other end against the sand with its paw. It pulled a length of meat free and wolfed it down in two great gulps.

As he approached on foot, Wheizer could see that the others were on the boat. The wizard kid and his red-haired older companion were in the mesquite thicket in the distance. He decided it would be much easier to eavesdrop on the pair at the thicket. He stayed at a low crouch, using outcroppings of sage and cactus as cover as he moved northeast. In the distance, he could see the pair starting to return from the thicket, each carrying a bundle of firewood as the daylight continued to fade. Wheizer hunkered down in a large growth of sage brush and shifted into rat form. Leaving his clothing and rapier well hidden in the brush, he moved to intercept the two.

He was hiding under a large prickly pear cactus when they passed by, one to the left and the other to the right of him. "What you done today... convincing them kids..." the red-headed man was saying. "That showed that you got the instinct of a great leader." The boy did not respond as they continued walking toward the camp.

Wheizer followed along cautiously, darting from cover to cover to stay in earshot of their discussion. Only they weren't very talkative. Then out of the nowhere, the man turned around and started walking backwards. Wheizer froze. He had cover from some sage brush... or did he?

"Eight days. Seven, maybe," the red-headed man said. Wheizer was confused, but then he understood. The man was looking at the waxing moon. He was talking about Mallet.

The boy said nothing in response, and the man turned and resumed walking toward the boat. Only the slightest hint of daylight remained.

The red-headed man froze in his tracks so suddenly that the boy ran into the back of him. "What? What is it?" the boy asked. The man was looking around intensely, with a finger held to his lips.

"What's wrong?" the boy whispered.

The man mouthed a word at the boy. What did he say? Wheizer couldn't make it out. He had some fair skill reading lips, but the light was not good and neither was his angle. The two were badly spooked. Had they guessed he was there? The boy mouthed something back. *"What does it mean?"* That is what it looked like to Wheizer, at least. The two stood stock still. The silence was intense; except for the distant sound of desert crickets, there was no sound at all. That's when Wheizer realized... there were no chirping crickets nearby! That is what had spooked the red-headed man. *"Crickets,"* had been the word he mouthed at the boy. He shrugged at the boy and resumed walking.

"Yeah. Eight days more I reckon 'til the full moon," the man said. What did he suspect?

The blasted crickets had given him away. His rat form was unnatural lycanthropy and the little blighters could sense him.

His rat form was no good. It would give him away. He'd have to stay in human form, but that made for much more risk. As soon as the two had moved another fifty or so yards away, he turned and scampered back to the sagebrush that hid his clothes. He'd have to creep up to their camp in human form if he hoped to learn anything from them.

It was well after dark. Four of the travelers sat talking around a campfire. Mallet must still be on the boat. Wheizer had positioned himself about twenty yards due south of them. Fortunately, a breeze was blowing from the north and that would both mask his scent from their dog and would help to carry their voices to him. In rat form, he could get right up in a bush next to them and hear everything perfectly, but that wasn't an option.

On the bright side, they didn't suspect him. They seemed convinced that someone was trying to scry them magically; as if a wizard would waste himself on these kids. Nevertheless, it worked to his advantage.

It wasn't worth the risk of creeping in closer yet as they jabbered on about stuff like stars, idle speculation about the sinkhole and the best way to wash a dish. He caught most of the conversation with occasional words being too faint or muffled to hear. But soon enough he caught the words "moss" and "Bystle Vale." He began to creep up quietly. He wanted to hear all the details he could. They had finally begun to talk about their destination. If he knew where they were going, he could get there first and wait for them. From what Wheizer could hear, it was a six- or seven-day journey by boat, and then another day or so on foot to the Bystle Vale. By air, it would only take a day or two. He'd have plenty of time to scout out this vale and get a good lay of the land.

The red-headed man stood up abruptly and headed to the boat with a lantern. Wheizer thought it best to stop moving to see what happened. Soon he came back, leading a bandaged

Mallet, no doubt recovering from the thrashing Wheizer had given him in the Mausoleum. Considering what he himself had been through in the last several days, it was hard to feel much sympathy for the boy. After all, it had been Mallet that knocked him off the lift.

Wheizer started creeping up again, slowly. They were discussing something given to them from someone called "Boxxaway", apparently the wizard boy's grandfather; a message, presumably. They talked about a bunch of nonsense, but eventually the boy got to reading the message. Wheizer continued to creep forward, ever so slowly. It was clear from the letter that they had to make a stop in the swamp, but their ultimate destination was someone called "Tharchelon." The letter mentioned moss several times, and it was clear that it was tremendously important. Probably valuable. His job was bringing Mallet home, and Brynn too, if it happened to work out. But what was the harm in making a little money on the side while he was at it? It seemed there was quite a bit more to learn about this moss.

Wheizer continued to inch forward.

"We are close," the red-headed man said. "We'll get there tomorrow. I reckon the wind looks promising."

"Someone is coming!" the girl suddenly said in an excited hiss. Wheizer froze. Surely she couldn't mean him?

The Agrabi whelp started to ask a question when the ground around Wheizer erupted in a shower of sparks. They weren't hot, but they startled him badly.

What in damnation was going on? Had he cried out when the sparks erupted? He couldn't be sure, but his instinct kicked in and he tore off toward Valsipherus at a full run. He had a head start, and the cover of darkness. Plus, he was fast. Wererats were known for their speed, even in human form.

Luckily, he evaded them. They had to stop for light to follow his tracks. He was able to make it back to where he had tied Valsipherus. The beast was calm, right where he had left him. He had been well-trained by the Demon's Bluff militia.

He flew southward, hugging the water. He could head back and report to Dagorn... no. He could handle this. Not even a minor setback. After all, he didn't think he'd been seen. Af ter about a mile, he started to climb and banked north to get ahead of the travelers and find this Bystle Vale they had talked about. As he passed by them high and to the east, he could see that they were too spooked to stay there for the night. They were breaking camp as he flew by.

9ᵗʰ Day of Summer – 7:00 PM – The Bystle Vale - 6 Days to the Full Moon

The vale hadn't been hard to find. The only question was whether it lay to the east or west of the river. Wheizer spotted it less than a half a day's walk to the east of the river gorge, high on the plateau. It was unmistakably the place, and was quite a sight from the air. It was a secluded little vale, surrounded by hills; a patchwork of farms and fields for goats and sheep. Five little Rothkin villages were scattered around the valley. A picturesque stream bisected the vale flowing east to west. But none of that was notable compared to the massive tree that grew near the center of the vale. The huge trunk stretched hundreds of feet into the air, creating an incredible canopy of large roundish leaves. It was hard to tell in the daylight, but it certainly seemed as if the fruits that hung from the branches were glowing.

It'd be a hell of a place to retire to... except for all the Rothkin. Clearly they'd have to go. How many Rothkin might there be here? Two thousand? Three? More? It would take barges and barges to cart them all down to the slave markets in Balankov...

He'd found the vale, but the question was, what to do now? It would probably be five or six days before Mallet and his companions arrived. Plenty of time to kill. Exploring the vale seemed the likely course of action, but it seemed unwise to just go wandering about as a human. As near as he could tell from the air, only Rothkin could be seen.

One thing was for sure, it would take a long time to cover all that ground in rat form. Wheizer decided to wait for nightfall so he could explore in human form. It wasn't hard to stay unseen, despite the fruits which indeed were glowing. There were plenty of wooded areas at the edge of most of the fields, and it was easy to move about without attracting attention. He had plenty of opportunity to listen in on conversations. The Rothkin had a peculiar accent, and they used an odd choice of words now and again but otherwise were understandable. There was much talk of weather and farming. Some talk of politics and something about a barrier, but not a single mention of moss. For something so seemingly important, these little folk spoke of it not at all. That led him to speculation on where the moss might be.

When morning came, he hid his clothes and shifted into rat form. He got up close to the big tree to investigate it, and to his surprise, Rothkin passed to and fro through heavily guarded and peculiar doors that led into the heart of the great tree trunk. Perhaps the moss was to be found inside the great tree. He didn't doubt that he could have sneaked in in rat form, but the odds of staying unseen seemed thin. He had gotten glimpses inside and there were inward-growing branches heavy with the glowing fruits. The interior was well-lit. A mouse, perhaps, could have gone unnoticed; but a large rat? Risky.

And suppose he found the moss? He knew from hard experience that he couldn't carry much in rat form. He couldn't likely walk out in human form, stark naked, holding big fistfuls of the stuff.

No... better to wait for Needle and Mallet and their friends to get the moss. Much easier to take it from them.

He had spent a full night and a day in the vale. He took the opportunity to sample the glowing fruits and found the taste sweet, but foreign. The glowing flesh had a sickeningly sweet smell. It reminded him of the mash at the rum distillers in Taglyon. When night came, he retrieved his clothes and shifted into human form to leave the vale. As he made his way along the wooded areas that bordered the fields, he surprised a filthy sheep herder that had stepped into the woods to relieve himself. His visage was of utter shock upon seeing a human walking through the vale. Wheizer speculated that he was the first big person this old shepherd had ever seen. The little man was about to call out when Wheizer stopped the cry short in the man's throat with his rapier. The blade had penetrated right at the bulge of his voice box. He didn't look as surprised in death as he had upon first seeing Wheizer. That was some manner of satisfaction to Wheizer. One dead, another two or three thousand to go. It was a start.

14ᵗʰ Day of Summer - 8:00 PM – Eastern Plateau – 1 Day to the Full Moon

It had been a relaxing couple of days, and Wheizer made the best of it. He had speared enough fish from the stream to feed himself, with plenty left over for Valsipherus. He'd made a makeshift hammock and a little smokeless cook fire off where a stream fed the reservoir above the dam. It was a rare opportunity to simply do nothing, and he reveled in every minute of it. After two days, he started making aerial patrols twice a day, looking for the boat heading up the gorge. Last night, he spotted them. The boat was sailing slowly upriver. He doubted they'd try to make the ascent up the wall of the gorge at night, but he'd be ready for them first thing in the morning, just in case.

*15th Day of Summer - 5:00 AM – Eastern Plateau – 17 Hours to
the Full Moon*

To his surprise, the kids did decide to make the climb in the
darkness of the early morning. There was just enough moonlight for him to see the boat beached at the bottom of the gorge.
The red-headed man remained behind on the boat with his dog
while the four kids started their journey to the top.

Wheizer spotted a perfect perch on the branch of a bristle-
cone pine tree. From there, he would have a good view of the
entire clearing and the edge of the gorge. He stripped down and
crammed the bundle of clothes between the trunk and branch
he'd chosen. He shifted into rat form and scrambled out to the
perfect overlook.

Just on the other side of the path, he noticed an old tower
with a large stone obelisk in front of it. Some ancient ruin from
olden times, by the look of it. No craftsman of today's age built
with such ability. Not that he was a stonemason, but Wheizer
liked to think he had an eye for quality.

After an hour or so, by the pre-dawn light, Wheizer spotted the oddest thing. A Rothkin sneaked into the clearing from
the south, passing quite near his tree. There was something
extremely disconcerting about the little man. He had pale skin,
and long, black hair. What was more, he was heavily-muscled
and had bony spikes protruding from his back, shoulders and
elbows. Bizarre tattoos covered his face and neck. He walked
with a sort of empty gait, and didn't move his head from side to
side. He had a badly deformed and oversized left hand. Wheizer
caught a whiff of his odor: sour milk.

Without a sound, the muscled Rothkin skulked right past
the obelisk into an open archway at the base of the ruined
tower and disappeared from view.

What in the infernal hells is going on?

Wheizer couldn't have been more surprised if an old tooth-
less whore from Balankov had sauntered into the clearing.

After another half hour or so, just after daybreak, a movement at the tree line on the eastern edge of the clearing caught
Wheizer's eye.

It was another Rothkin.

This one looked normal. He was trying to remain unseen, but wasn't doing an adequate job of it. It seemed Wheizer was not the only one intent on watching the comings and goings in this clearing.

Not long after he spotted the second Rothkin, Mallet emerged from the trail at the top of the cliff. He had healed up nicely. The rest of them emerged, including Needle. Wheizer couldn't resist a smile at the thought of the fun he'd had with Needle the last few weeks, but seeing Mallet gave him a rush of feelings he wasn't used to experiencing. He'd always liked the boy, but now Wheizer felt a deeper connection with him. Was it like the connection between father and son? No. It was more than that.

"You guys got to look at this," Needle said, looking over the edge of the precipice.

"Look," Brynn exclaimed, pointing up the gorge.

It was clear from their ensuing discussion that they were talking about a large crack in the dam. Meanwhile, he noticed that the Rothkin at the edge of the clearing had disappeared and there was no sign from the unnatural creature in the tower.

Eventually, Needle led them toward that selfsame tower, proclaiming it the Tower of Rovule. Wheizer didn't care what it might have been called or what it might have contained, but he did care about the gangly creature within. Wheizer knew a cold-blooded killer when he saw one, and he grew slightly concerned lest the creature kill Needle and spoil his plans for selling him into a long life of servitude.

At the same time, Wheizer also noticed that a few Rothkin warriors had quietly begun to arrive at the eastern edge of the clearing. They were moving with the intent not to be seen. The four kids were completely oblivious to their arrival.

Needle started off toward the tower, seemingly intent on investigating it. He hadn't quite gotten to the obelisk when a flock of small birds exploded out of the tower in a chittering cacophony. The unnatural Rothkin sauntered out of the archway into plain view of the four.

Well now... Wheizer thought, *this could be a problem.*

The creature walked forward, his normal hand holding a

black ball about the size of large cherry. He held it before him as if taunting the four of them, though his tattooed face showed no expression at all. As the creature walked forward, Wheizer noticed something very peculiar. The rising sun was casting long shadows from the pines east of the clearing. There were patches where the bright beams of the morning sun peeked through among the shadows. The creature made the slightest side-steps and adjustments to carefully avoid the direct sunlight. *He's sticking to the shadows!*

Needle stopped dead in his tracks and then slowly started to back away. Something odd began to happen. The branch Wheizer perched upon was transmitting strong vibrations up from the ground. A block of stone broke free from the top of the ruined tower and started to fall.

It was another earthquake.

The ground suddenly heaved violently and the four kids struggled to keep their balance. The unnatural Rothkin was almost knocked over and hunkered in reaction.

A thunder crack shattered the air and the earthquake intensified. The unnatural-looking Rothkin was having severe difficulties and was completely unbalanced. He didn't notice the nearby obelisk wobbling dangerously, but Needle noticed it. Just as the obelisk was starting to tip, Needle raced forward and shoved the distracted Rothkin directly into the path of the falling obelisk. It crushed him, pinning most of him under the weight of the stone.

Impressive. Needle was full of surprises. There was a part of Wheizer that really admired Needle. His life had been hard, but it had made him strong. In a lot of ways, Needle reminded him of himself as a boy. It might have been a mistake to have rejected him as an initiate in the Demon's Bluff Thieves Guild. He might have developed into a real asset.

On the other hand, he was a filthy Agrabi whelp and what was worse, he was Kemano's son. Hadn't Wheizer promised to sell him into slavery? *Well, a promise is a promise.*

The ground had stopped shaking, but there was still a tremendous roar coming from the gorge. It sounded to Wheizer like a torrent of running water. Had the dam broken?

Cael grabbed the black sphere the creature had dropped as

Mallet stepped forward and went to work with his glaive. The creature's head should have been cleaved in two with Mallet's first blow, but it barely put a nick on his scalp. Then the creature began to lift the massive stone off himself. Even Wheizer in the rabid grip of full moon fever wouldn't have been able to accomplish such a feat, especially considering the lack of leverage. *The creature was unnatural indeed.*

The boy, Cael, fired some sort of beam of magical light at the creature from his finger, and he reacted as if he'd been stung by a desert scorpion. The boy's spell had hurt him... no... it was the *light* from the boy's spell. Had any of them noticed? Doubtful.

The creature continued to try to lift the huge stone and it looked like he just might succeed. Mallet had jumped up onto the great rock, but it didn't help much. If Wheizer was going to save his new progeny, he'd have to do something... but he dare not reveal himself, especially with the little Rothkin army gathered at the edge of the clearing.

Wheizer scampered back along the branch to where his clothes were stuffed. Luckily the hilt of his rapier protruded. He took it in his mouth and dragged it back along the branch. In rat form, it was difficult to manipulate, but he managed to catch a spot of sunlight with the shiny guard above the hilt and reflect it toward the creature.

Just as he expected, the creature reacted. The problem was that the kids were so involved that none of them noticed. Wheizer tried reflecting the light into Mallet's eyes, but the big boy was too engaged in his struggle. Wheizer shifted to Needle and the Agrabi boy looked his way with a squint. Wheizer directed the light again to the creature. It didn't take Needle long. Damn! If only Mallet had the Agrabi whelp's instincts.

Needle scampered up a nearby pine tree and pushed the branches apart, bathing the unholy creature in a bright, unbroken beam of streaming sunlight. The monster screamed an unearthly howl and disappeared in a puff of black smoke.

Fortunately for Wheizer, they got distracted by the thundering sound from the chasm and ended up gawking over the edge before Needle could remember to investigate the true source of their salvation.

From their reaction looking down the gorge, it was clear that the dam had indeed broken. One thing was for sure, he wouldn't want to be in Demon's Bluff when that flood hit. On the bright side, the Kuma could use a good scrubbing.

The group of Rothkin from the eastern edge of the clearing started walking toward them. They were led by one who stood a full head taller than the rest. His face was covered with bruises and scabs. Wheizer took note. He had the feral look of a real fighter.

None of the children noticed the approaching Rothkin as they were too preoccupied with the flood in the gorge. If the Rothkin had chosen to attack at that moment, they would have made short work of the four. But instead, the leader cleared his throat loudly after they passed by the fallen obelisk.

Wheizer had chosen his vantage well. He was perfectly positioned in the right place at the right time to overhear everything and this had all the markers of an important meeting. He nestled himself comfortably on the branch with a self-satisfied sigh.

The four kids were all completely surprised. After the two groups sized each other up for a few moments, the brown-haired kid stepped forward and said "My... my name is Cael Hotheway. We come seeking an audience with King Tharchelon."

A very interesting conversation ensued...

Wheizer continued to listen to the discussion, which carried on for some time. It was quite enlightening, and explained a lot of *what* they were doing, but did little to explain *why*. Clearly, Mallet and Brynn had gotten themselves mixed up in Elowynn and Kemano's schemes. From the events in the mausoleum, it was clear that Brynn had begun to dabble in

Elowynn's witchcraft. Troubling indeed.

As he suspected, the moss was of great value. The Rothkin said it was the source of the magic in the vale and was somehow connected to the huge tree he had seen. Also, as he suspected, the moss was located inside the trunk of the huge tree. That the moss was magical definitely expanded the potential market. There were dozens of wizards in Demon's Bluff that would likely have an interest, and there was no shortage of wealth among them.

They haggled over the moss at length. The king expected three of those little black orbs, but the kids had only the one. He used that fact as leverage to reel them into some complicated plot to get them to do his bidding.

It all sounded overly complex. Wheizer suspected that nothing the king said was true. What his motivation might be was unknowable, but Wheizer knew deception and manipulation when he saw it.

One fascinating note was a revelation by Cael that he had seen a Rothkin snooping around his house back in Demon's Bluff. Surely it was the same Rothkin that was trying to kill them in the Mausoleum... before Wheizer had put a stop to that. That seemed a more plausible explanation for how the Rothkin King knew their names. He might have had spies in Demon's Bluff watching them for quite a while. Some part of Wheizer wanted to unravel the reasons and motives of all involved, but that was an absurd indulgence. None of that really mattered. He had only one objective, and that was to bring Mallet back. If he could get some of that moss in the bargain, so much the better.

The right time to intervene with Mallet would be at the full moon tonight. That is when he'd have some leverage with Mallet, and the boy would be in the right frame of mind to go along willingly.

Needle suddenly got disruptive and accused the King of lying. The kid was smart enough to know they were being played and he had sand, but the straight-out accusation probably wasn't the smartest move. Needle managed to get himself under the King's skin even before the smear on his integrity. He certainly had a talent for that.

The King whistled for his warriors to return and proceeded to beat the hells out of Cael, Needle and even Mallet, in a surprisingly impressive display of puissance. The fact that Mallet could be beaten by Tharchelon made Wheizer take note. Best not to underestimate the little fellow.

He also wondered if he should intervene, but decided to let events play out. Besides, the beating was quite entertaining. It ended with the four of them hogtied.

The King, realizing that his lies had failed to convince, decided upon a more direct means. He would hold Needle hostage, forcing the other three to do his bidding.

They sent Needle marching off to the northeast with a small group of Rothkin warriors and the rest headed off directly to the east, the direction of the vale. What to do? One thing was for sure... the king had every intention of killing all four of them as soon as he was done with them.

While his first responsibility was to Mallet, going after Mallet's group directly seemed unwise. There were so many Rothkin guards, and they were clearly capable fighters despite their diminutive size. He'd likely have a better chance of rescuing Needle, and then at least he'd have some help. Besides, he already knew how to get to the vale, where Mallet's group were headed. He had no idea where they were taking Needle.

It was decided. As soon as it was safe, he climbed down, shifted into a man and got dressed. He headed in the direction they had taken Needle.

15th Day of Summer - 2:00 PM – The Barrier – 8 Hours Until the Full Moon

Wheizer pushed against the invisible barrier again as Needle disappeared into the underbrush. He hated not being in control of a situation, but there was no helping it in this case. He couldn't get into the vale. There was no real hope of communicating with them inside, either. He'd have to hope they would come out *before* the full moon. That was all there was to it. If they didn't, there were only two likely outcomes. They would all get killed by the Rothkin, or Mallet would survive and be an unusable, emotional wreck. The former seemed much more likely than the latter as he gamed out the possibilities. Dagorn wouldn't be happy with either, but the latter was the better option. It all boiled down to them coming out before the full moon, with or without that moss.

He'd need a vantage point that gave him the best opportunity to spot them as they exited... *if* they exited. He had to assume they would come out somewhere on this western side. If they came out somewhere else, he'd never find them. Then it hit him; he had the perfect means of finding them wherever they exited... even before they got close to the barrier! Ha! His new strategy still wasn't foolproof, but it gave him some measure of control. He allowed himself a smile as he turned away from the invisible barrier to fetch Valsipherus.

CHAPTER SEVEN
The Bystle Tree

"We were baffled by how the Cult's mages circumvented the cost of casting. It turns out their mages paid a far heavier cost."

- Gadrax Von Torinovo

15th Day of Summer – 3:30 PM – The Bystle Tree – About 7 Hours Until the Full Moon

Cael stood frozen, stunned by the violence. The red-haired Rothkin in the back turned the large crossbow straight at Cael. The weapon emitted white puffs of smoke. He could hear a sizzling sound; the smell of burnt hair and roasted meat filled his nostrils. He immediately understood that the gunner had used the crossbow to fire magical lightning at Chetelar, their guide, whose headless corpse lay at his feet, blood burbling from his neck into the black loam.

Nothing in his experience prepared him to confront such a terrifying weapon of war. The militia of Demon's bluff had erected mighty trebuchets atop the plateau to defend the city from attack. They even had an aerie with a few dozen trained Gryphons they used as aerial mounts. But he had seen neither force in action.

Cael raised his hands into the air, wincing. He could feel his wounded right hand shaking like he had the palsy. Brynn and Mallet, standing to either side of him, raised their hands as well. Apparently no one wanted to suffer Chetelar's fate.

Would their quick surrender save them? The gunner looked way too eager. Would he just finish them off right now without bothering to find out who they were?

Desperately, Cael began pulling in the peculiar magical energy of the vale. He had been experimenting all afternoon by gathering the strange energy into his bones and spiraling it into his stomach. It was a weird, oily energy. It felt slippery, and wouldn't stay in his belly like the energy of the *Arcanus Navitas.*

Would it work? Would it power a spell? He was about to find out when out of nowhere a pair of scrawny, olive-skinned arms swung a makeshift wooden club from behind the flyer. The club smashed into the fruit impaled on the spike and it exploded, sending wet chunks and fragments in all directions.

A wave of energy washed over Cael, causing him to take a wild step back, lowering his arms. Strangely, neither Mallet nor Brynn seemed to feel the pulse, and stood solid.

The flyer dropped from its low hover with a 'klunk'. The two Rothkin cried out with high-pitched yelps. To Cael's utter astonishment, Raju 'Needle' Graji himself leaped onto the rear of the flying machine, wielding the club. The gunner spun around wildly, frantically pulling the trigger on his crossbow, but nothing happened.

Needle winked at Cael, his lips pulled back in a feral grin. He swung his club at the gunner's head. There was a sickening crunch as the heavy wood split the red-haired Rothkin's forehead wide open. The gunner slumped down, either dead or unconscious.

Meanwhile, the pilot had quickly unfastened himself from his restraints. Needle stepped around the gunner and just as the pilot turned to stand, Needle's club smashed into his upturned face. The Rothkin slumped back into his seat.

Needle hopped down off the flyer as a stiff breeze kicked up and stirred the high canopy of the tree, rustling the leaves. He had a leather sack tied shut and strapped over his left shoulder. He walked up and stood before Cael.

Cael felt the oily energy drain from his body, and wondered if his spell would have succeeded. He turned his focus to Needle and was about to greet him when he noticed the Agrabi boy's face and recoiled. Needle must have recently suffered a savage beating. Purple bruises and red raspberry scratches covered his cheeks, chin, and chest.

"What in hells happened to you?" Cael blurted.

"And how did you escape?" Brynn added incredulously, walking up to him and reaching out a tentative hand to a particularly large egg-sized lump above his eyebrow.

Needle swatted her hand away.

"Nice work there," Mallet said, pointing with his chin to the disabled flyer and its crew.

"Are they dea—,"

Thunk! An arrow cut off Brynn's question, embedding itself into the loam at their feet, the fletching still vibrating. As one, they raised their heads and looked up. The tree was impossibly tall. There were catwalks along the branches and little bridges that crossed from branch to branch. Cael estimated the lowest catwalks were at least several hundred feet up. The tiny head and shoulders of a Rothkin archer peered down at them over the edge of a platform. There were several such platforms up in the branches. Cael could see two more of the strange flying machines perched upon them. The archer who had fired at them gave a shout and nocked another arrow.

Cael flung himself against the tree, flattening his body. Mallet grabbed Brynn, pushing her close to the huge exposed root. He covered her protectively. Needle followed suit, hugging the wood.

The second arrow missed, thunking into the earth inches from Cael's foot. He flinched, hugging the tree even more closely. He had already taken a stab wound through the hand.... He didn't like how close that arrow had come to giving him a mirror wound in his foot. The keen sense of his own mortal peril overwhelmed Cael's senses.

Distant cries of alarm erupted from far above them. Rothkin warriors were racing along the catwalks to join the first archer. Cael groped desperately inside his pocket for the ring Tharchelon had given him but it was far too small to fit on anything but the end of his pinkie. He slid it over his nail and held his breath as he quickly touched the ring to the section of exposed root that Chetelar had indicated.

It came alive. A vertical seam appeared upon the surface and cracked itself wide apart. The small opening led into a narrow tunnel beyond, formed into the wood of the giant root itself.

A warm, yellowish blush of light illuminated the tunnel within.

Cael didn't hesitate. He jumped through the secret portal. He was followed by the others as a volley of arrows thudded into the ground behind them. As soon as they were safe inside, the opening sealed itself shut with a snap.

Were the walls caving in on him? Or was it just really cramped in here?

"Can anyone breathe?" Cael asked.

"It's stuffy," Brynn acknowledged, rubbing her forehead. She had leapt through the portal and knocked into the opposite wall of the hallway. It was surprisingly confined.

"Mallet?" Cael asked, looking back. Hell, the big kid was nearly bent over double. His glaive was another challenge. Rather than hold it in his customary upright position, he had to hold it parallel to the ground.

Needle immediately tripped over it and frowned at Mallet, whose head was beading up with sweat droplets. Mallet didn't look so good.

Needle took a deep breath: "Air seems fine to me." He sidled away from the sharp metal glaive head and moved up next to Cael.

"Seems a little tight," Cael said.

"*Seems?*" Mallet coughed. "This is no good."

"Come on," said Needle, "We've been in worse than this. Remember Ganger's tomb, Cael?"

There was something about this place that was incredibly unsettling to Cael. Still, he didn't want the others to worry, so he smiled. "Yeah, we sure have, haven't we?"

"I'm having a hard time imagining a worse place," Mallet said, and he coughed again. "I think you're right, Cael, the air in here is thick."

Thick... that was a good way to describe it. The air was heavy, humid and just a bit too warm. Worse, the bastardized magic in this place was so... *greasy*... unnatural. Cael looked around, trying to get a sense of the place. The tunnel was lit by numerous yellow glowing fruits that hung from leafy branches growing inward at periodic intervals. The tunnel seemed to be shaped seamlessly from the very wood of the tree itself and was polished to a high sheen. Cael leaned over and looked into the beautiful grain of the golden-hued wood. Was that his reflection? Or was it something else?

"Are there faces in the wood?"

Brynn and Needle looked. Mallet didn't move, but started taking quick shallow breaths.

"I..." Brynn said.

"No..." said Needle playfully. "Wait... yes? Do you see something?"

"I don't know," she replied.

"Maybe it's the souls of the damned," Needle said. Brynn jumped back with a yelp.

"Quit teasing her," Cael said, feeling jumpy himself.

Cael sucked in another 'thick' breath of air. An odd, unfamiliar smell permeated the place. It was a warm and fruity odor that was nonetheless discomforting. It smelled a little like rotting apples.

"They'll be looking for us soon," Needle said, poking Cael.

Cael nodded. He needed to stay focused. They had a mission and their situation seemed tenuous at best. He pocketed Tharchelon's ring and took out the parchment map. Needle and Brynn gathered in close to have a look. Poor Mallet was out of luck from his stooped position. He groaned, coughing again.

The map made Cael's head spin. It was a maze of levels showing countless intertwining passageways and chambers. Thankfully, the moss garden was circled with red chalk. But how to get there? It required walking a path through this maze. How in the world would they do it without running into anyone?

"It was Wheizer," Needle said suddenly in a low voice.

"What?" Brynn asked, confused.

"Wheizer?" Mallet asked, whispering. "You saw Wheizer's face in the wood?"

"Not in the wood," Needle said, giving Mallet a disgusted glance.

"Wheizer..." said Cael. He looked at Needle, saw the bruises on his face. Could it be? Wheizer was here? He should be dead.

"Yeah, it was Wheizer," Needle said.

"Wheizer can't be here," said Brynn. "You killed him with the silver dagger. We all saw it."

"Yeah, yeah, I did see it, but damn Brynn... he healed," said Needle, shuddering. "I don't think silver automatically kills wererats." He glanced back at Mallet, fingered the hilt of his dagger.

This was interesting news, Cael thought. And... come to think of it, not entirely surprising. If Dagorn was in the Cult of Yex as they suspected, and Wheizer worked for him, it stood to reason Wheizer was coming for the moss.

Boxxaway had warned that the cult would want it, and perhaps the old man had underestimated their desire for it. Knowing what Cael knew now... he could see how handy the wretched stuff would be for them. Here was yet another thing to add to his worry list. Elija had been bad enough. Tharchelon wasn't much better. But adding Wheizer into the mix made this dangerous situation even pricklier. It really was getting hard to breathe in here.

"Hey," Needle whispered, signaling for Cael to bend his head close as they began walking down the tunnel. Cael was trying to trace a pattern through the tunnels that would take them in a roundabout way up to the Moss Garden.

"What if he rats out in here?" Needle whispered, pointing back over his shoulder with his thumb to Mallet. "We won't stand a chance."

Cael nodded, whispering back: "If we are still in this tree by the time the moon rises, we are all dead anyway. Keep your silver dagger ready." Needle shot him a worried look. Cael shared it also. Any hope that Needle's silver dagger would secure their safety when Mallet shape shifted now seemed far-fetched and even naïve.

"Remember, Wheizer survived that fall from the lifts, too," Mallet added absently, unaware they had just been talking about him.

"But how could he be here?" Brynn asked. "It doesn't make any sense."

"Somehow he knew we were coming here," said Needle. "And he got here ahead of us. He knows about the moss. He thinks it is worth a lot of money... thinks he can sell it to the wizards on the cliff."

"He is working for your father, Brynn," said Cael as he stopped at a four-way intersection. "Of course, Dagorn wants the Moss." He stared at the map for a moment and rotated it in his hands, looking down each hallway.

"We don't know that my father is part of the Cult of Yex," Brynn said.

"Ehh...." Mallet said from behind, "How else do you possibly explain it, Brynn?"

Needle stepped up and pointed on the parchment. "We go right," he said confidently.

Cael led the way. His mouth was dry and he was suddenly thirsty.

"Wheizer freed you from the Rothkin?" asked Brynn. "Why would he do that?"

"Not quite what happened," said Needle. "They had me tied up in some camp. Wheizer snuck in and untied me. He brought me to the vale to help find the three of you. I think he's looking for Mallet. He beat the hells out of me in the process. He didn't know about the barrier, though. It let me through, but it stopped him cold. You should have seen the look on his face."

"So where is he now?" Brynn asked.

Needle shrugged. "Out there waiting for us. He wants the moss, so I expect he aims to take it from us if we manage to get out of here with it."

"Just like Tharchelon," Cael said.

"This is out of order," Brynn added.

"It makes perfect sense, Brynn," said Cael. "You just don't want to believe your father is a part of the Cult of Yex."

"You are right," she sighed. "I don't. I don't. There are a lot of things I'd prefer not to believe, Cael."

"Shhh!" Needle hissed. They all stopped short. They heard the sound of Rothkin voices and boots from far behind them.

"What do we do now?" asked Needle.

"There is no way I can turn around," Mallet said, down on one knee.

Cael looked at the map of the inside of the tree. "We need to find a place to hide!"

"Up and to the left," Needle said, jabbing a dirty finger onto the map. Cael nodded and ran as quickly as he could, banging his head on the ceiling more than once as he turned right, then left.

"Your hiding place," Needle said, as he pointed to a large, discolored section of wood. As Cael touched the door with the ring, the wood creaked opened as a vertical seam appeared.

He paused and looked at Needle as Brynn and Mallet finally arrived. "What is in there?"

"It's a storeroom," Needle said. "According to the map."

"Shhh..." Cael said, looking at Mallet. His breathing was making enough noise that he was pretty sure the whole tree could hear them.

"In," Mallet said, looking back the way they had come.

Cael nodded and entered the opening. In short order, they were inside and the portal closed behind them.

The room was dark with only a faint hint of a yellowish glow that left everything indistinct. Cael smelled a strong musty odor. Brynn's sandstone suddenly illuminated the room in its eerie blue light. Cael winced. He would never get used to those strange witch lights. He simply could not understand where the power came from.

He looked around. If Cael thought the tunnels were tight, this new room was another matter entirely. Cramped was a generous word. They were alone in some sort of storage room. Racks against the wall held countless bottles that were the source of the faint yellowish glow. The rest of the low-ceilinged room was filled with casks, crates and burlap sacks filled with what Cael assumed was grain. Thin nets held onions in bunches and hung from the ceiling along with what looked like garlic cloves, bundles of dried herbs and many dozen shanks of dried meat. There was a large pile of smallish potatoes next to an even larger pile of dried mushrooms.

Needle's eyes went wide at all the food. He snatched a mushroom from the pile and brought it to his nose. "Ooof," he said, pulling it away from his nose quickly. "This place brings new meaning to the term 'root cellar'." He then popped the mushroom into his mouth and chewed. "Not as bad as it smells."

Cael frowned at Needle as Mallet put his ear to the wall through which they had entered. "I can't hear anything," he mouthed a whisper. He was sweating profusely.

Cael nodded and coughed. The dry mustiness made the stuffy air in the hall seem positively inviting by comparison.

Needle headed directly over to the rack of bottles and grabbed one, pulling the cork out with his teeth. "What do you suppose this is?" he asked, giving it a swig.

"Shh..." Brynn whispered furiously at him.

The Agrabi boy swallowed and smiled. Cael could see the faint yellowish glow on his teeth and tongue.

"Needle!" Brynn hissed. "You don't know what that is!"

"It's some kind of wine, I think," he said as he took another larger drink. "Made from their glow fruits, not grapes. Cael, let me see the map, I want to look at it."

Cael handed it over and watched as Needle studied it by the faint light of the Bystle Wine.

"This is interesting..." said Needle.

"Shh..." Mallet whispered. He signaled violently to the door. Was someone outside? Then Cael heard the footsteps *right outside the door.* He tried to hold his breath, felt a sudden tickle in the back of his throat.

He caught Mallet's gaze. Cael raised his sleeve into his lowered face and let a soft cough out into the fabric.

Did the footsteps pause?

There was a muffled sneeze behind him... Cael turned. Needle had sneezed into his arm. The smaller boy looked abashed, bent over low trying to stifle a second sneeze.

They all held still. Cael felt his skin suddenly start to crawl. The confining oppression made him want to kick and scream. He had been slowly gathering power but now the greasy energy of the tree was starting to slip from him. He closed his eyes, facing the door, ready to unleash a spell of destruction...

He rubbed his left wrist absently and felt the scarring from where he had sliced his wrist. He allowed himself a brief moment to relish the vision of his mother's beautiful face. The vision he would never forget...

There was a gluck-gluck-gluck sound Cael was vaguely

aware of. And some whispered swearing... Was it Needle? He didn't care anymore... He started to shake, remembering the feeling of being in the closet, watching himself be born, unaware at first he was looking through the eyes of the very assassin that would shortly murder both his father and mother...

Thank the heavens Boxxaway had been there to save him.

I wish I had never seen that, Cael thought. Of all things to have to witness. Father... assassin... Mother... Only a glimpse of his beautiful mother... but only a glimpse was enough to fill his heart totally full, despite the horror of what had happened next. If only that angelic vision hadn't been followed by the murderous, hellish blade. Cael realized that the short vision he'd seen through the Lorgnettes had contained both the best and worst memories of his life. Why couldn't he simply have the good without the bad?

Cael felt like his heart was skipping beats. The air in the room felt like it was being siphoned off by the panic in each of them...

The sound of footsteps in the hall started to retreat.

He felt a thump in his chest... yes... yes, his heart was beating again... he sipped in some of the dank air.

"What should we do now?" Mallet asked, poking the door with a shaky finger. "I think they went by and missed us. Do we get back after it, or give them some time to settle down?"

Was there any real choice? "I think we have to keep going," said Cael. He could not remain long in this room. "They know we are inside and are probably just doing a quick search now, thinking they will find us easily. It won't take them long to come back and search more thoroughly."

Mallet and Brynn nodded their agreement.

They looked to Needle, who had a stricken look on his face.

Cael felt his breath catch again. "What?"

Needle handed Cael the map. Cael look down at it. He lost all his breath. Needle had spilled the glowing wine all over it. More than half of the map was smeared and unreadable.

"What in the infected hells are we going to do now?" Mallet asked, his eyes large and panicked. What little air remained was getting quickly sucked into his flaring nostrils.

"We'll figure it out," Cael said calmly, though he didn't believe his own words for a second. How could they find the Moss Garden now? With guards out there searching for them, they were in deep trouble with no map.

Needle grinned. "I got us all taken care of."

Cael bit down. He had been slowly overcoming a strong dislike of Needle over the last two weeks, and had even grown to respect him. But right now, hearing him shrug off his careless stupidity, he felt a rising enmity, if not momentary hatred, of the Agrabi boy.

Needle immediately understood Cael's look and put both hands up, "No, really!" he said quickly. "We're okay. I've got the map memorized... basically."

"The whole map?" Brynn asked.

"Yes!" he said. "I did. I can do that. Tell them, Cael."

Cael found his breath again. Needle might have a remarkable sense of direction... but he didn't believe he could memorize the map in just a few seconds. "You can lead us to the Moss Garden?"

"I know I can," Needle said reassuringly. "Come on, I'll show you. It's all up here." He tapped his noggin.

Cael shook his head. He motioned for Mallet to step away from the door so he could open it with the ring.

Needle took one last pull of the glowing liquid and set his bottle down. "We are still below ground, inside the roots," he said. "There is a flight of stairs just near here. We can start climbing toward the Moss Garden."

"Root cellar!" Mallet exclaimed suddenly.

"What?" Brynn asked.

"Because it's in the roots!"

Needle started to open his mouth. "Nah," he said. "Too easy."

Needle led them from the storage room through labyrinthine tunnels. They followed him up seven or eight flights of stairs without being detected, though they had to detour and hide twice to avoid noises ahead of them. Once, they hid for what must have been hours. It sounded like a search of the whole tree was being conducted. They only escaped discovery by hiding in an abandoned room piled with crates, cloaked in the shadows of Brynn's darkening sigil.

Cael was developing a respect for Needle with every level that they navigated successfully, but still he doubted. They were climbing, yes, but had they reached the Moss Garden? For all he knew, they could be nowhere near it.

But just when he thought they were going to get through unscathed, their luck ran out. They turned a corner and came upon a single Rothkin warrior standing watch silently. The little bastard yelled at the top of his lungs, and ran toward them.

The shock caused Cael and Needle both to backpedal, but the heretofore-shaky Mallet suddenly came alive, raised the head of his glaive, and charged forward to meet their attacker.

Needle, Brynn, and Cael flattened themselves to the side of the round tunnel as Mallet charged by them. The blade of his glaive came uncomfortably close to Cael's stomach, and Mallet's shoulder dealt him a glancing blow as he rambled past, a low growl rumbling from his throat.

To Cael's utter amazement, the Rothkin stopped short at the spectacle of the huge boy thundering at him, turned, and fled. Mallet pursued.

"Stop!" Cael called as Mallet disappeared around a corner.

"The idiot," Needle said. They looked at each other. What to do now?

Before more than a moment passed, Mallet ambled back with a huge grin on his face and Cael smiled in relief.

"You see that?" Mallet asked. He seemed fully recovered from his claustrophobia.

"Yeah, okay," said Needle. "You *are* useful. Happy?" He slid past Mallet and led them again through the wooden halls. They navigated the route up several more flights of stairs until they came to a four-way intersection. Needle finally turned back to them. "*The garden is just ahead*," he mouthed almost silently.

Needle poked his head around the corner of the left hand passage, and pulled back quickly. "I think this is it," he whispered and signaled for Cael to take a look. Cael peeked around the corner.

The corridor widened and heightened considerably as it ran maybe sixty feet to a large, domed open space. The far wall had a curious arrangement of Bystle Fruits framing an ornate and curious doorway.

It sure looked like it was the entrance to something special. Unfortunately, standing in front of the doors was a group of at least ten armed Rothkin warriors. Their presence suggested Needle was right. It also suggested whoever was in charge was possibly expecting them and was guarding the Moss Garden.

He pulled back, explaining what he and Needle had seen to Mallet and Brynn. Mallet wasn't content to be told and took a look around the corner himself.

After a moment, Mallet stepped back and hefted his glaive. 'Don't see as we got any choice, yes?"

"But what if this isn't the Moss Garden?" asked Brynn. "We don't want to get into a fight for nothing."

"We could try and distract them," said Needle. "I can stand out there, call to them, and let them chase me."

"Or I could charge them and scare them off," Mallet said.

Cael considered. Fighting ten Rothkin didn't sound smart in the slightest, but neither did sending Needle off on his own with them chasing him, no matter how entertaining that might be. Either way, they had to act fast or they'd be discovered soon.

"Can you cast a spell and roast them to death in a blast of fire?" Needle asked.

"Aren't we in a wooden tree?" Mallet asked, looking at Needle like he was made of wood himself.

Cael felt a throb in his wrist. He wasn't sure if the foreign Bystle Magic even worked... but even if it did, the extent of his ability was to cast a small ball of fire. It might hurt one of them, but not ten...

He had a momentary vision of surprising the ten Rothkin in a fiery blast of heat and destruction.

"Or..." Mallet repeated, "I can just charge them first, and

Cael can save his magic for later. I think they will run when they see me, and if they don't... well, there is plenty of room for me to fight down there, and you haven't seen me fight yet. Those Rothkin aren't going to be a problem for me."

"Well..." said Needle. "They seemed to be a problem for you back at the tower."

"Yeah, but they surprised me," said Mallet. "This time they will be the ones surprised. And besides, Tharchelon isn't here."

"We have seen you fight," said Needle. "Remember Elija? And I agree with you, you should charge, we'll follow, and as soon as they run from your ugly face, we'll open the doors and sneak right on up and get us some moss."

Cael nodded, though he was still uncertain this was the right course of action. What if it wasn't the Moss Garden? Needle could be wrong. He was, after all, the idiot who had accidentally destroyed the map.

The ramifications of what they were about to do danced at the edge of Cael's mind. This fight might require them to kill these Rothkin. Perhaps Needle had already killed one or both on the flyer with his club, but Cael thought they would probably recover. He took a deep breath. What choice did they have now? He didn't want to hesitate and think about it any longer. It was time to act, right or wrong. He gathered the slippery Bystle Magic, held his knife ready, and signaled for Mallet to go.

Mallet grinned. He let out a roar as he ran around the corner and charged, using his glaive like a lance.

Cael swallowed hard, and followed.

The Rothkin guards did not run away. They stood stock still, frozen in terror. Mallet's glaive caught the nearest Rothkin guard full in the chest, slicing through the leather breastpiece and into his sternum. Cael watched, seemingly in slow motion, as the guard snapped backward.

Where the initial clash had seemed to slow the flow of time for Cael, the ensuing chaos seemed to move almost too quickly for him to track. The next Rothkin launched himself at the shaft of the glaive, grappling it before Mallet could withdraw it for another go. The weapon was so unwieldy that Mallet instinctively abandoned it, stepping forward to meet the onrushing gang of guards with his bare hands.

Mallet threw a punch with his massive, meaty fist, knocking another Rothkin backwards, but in the process he lost his balance, tripping forward over the Rothkin that had glommed onto his glaive. The guards were on him in a flash, grappling him in a vain effort to subdue him. One of the guards raised a short sword, the menacing point beginning a deadly plunge toward Mallet's unprotected shoulder. Mallet turned, throwing off one of the guards clinging to him, barely dodging the blow.

Needle arrived and plunged his dagger into the neck of the guard that Mallet had just tossed. Cael noticed one of the guards at the back of the group detach and flee down a side passage.

Cael began to shape the strange Bystle Magic into a spell. His initial idea was to use fire, but now he thought that might be a bad idea with Mallet and Needle in the middle of the melee, and this being a wooden tree and all. He abandoned that spell and started to form a different one.

The guard with the short sword retracted for another stab, but this time Mallet had a clear view of the attack. His hand shot up and grabbed the Rothkin by the forearm, arresting the forward motion of the blade before it reached his ribs. With a mighty twist of his wrist, Mallet snapped the guard's forearm to a disturbing angle; the cracking sound was startlingly loud. The guard cried out in agony, dropping his blade as Mallet hurled him against a wall. Needle quickly dispatched this one with his dagger, as well. Brynn stepped forward and grabbed the dropped short sword. She held it in front of her determinedly.

Two more guards rushed Mallet.

Cael's mind finally clicked on the right spell, his old standby. But he had never tried to *hold* anyone rushing at him, and he had never tried two simultaneous targets before.

To his surprise, the Bystle Magic, as slippery as it was, came out of his extended hands in roughly the form he needed. The wave of energy struck the two rushing guards. One of the guards tensed up and fell forward, paralyzed. The other was affected enough to fall forward, dazed. He quickly struggled back to his feet.

There was a brief moment of sweet elation as the energy flowed from him... and then a sudden drop... but that was it.

Nothing else. He was accustomed to the feel of just a tiny piece of his life force dripping out of his body and away forever no matter how small the spell he cast. Always with that feeling was the question of how many days had he just aged?

But not this time. There was no loss, there was no sense of aging... This was interesting... unexpected...

Needle pounced on the two fallen guards, killing the more mobile of the two first. His executions were fast and final; very little thought in them. In a weird way, they reminded Cael of the murder of his parents: quick, lethal and thoughtless. His heart constricted again.

He wasn't the only one. Needle looked up at him, his face twisted into a crinkled mess. Needle had no love or joy for the job he had done. His hands were shaking and he looked down and away, trying to hide his tears.

Between them, they had just killed several Rothkin. Cael had considered the implications before, but it was nothing compared to the reality of it, after the fact. He would have to set it aside and fret about it later. Too much was happening.

Two more guards fled down the small side hallway following their first cowardly companion. They were screaming. It wouldn't be long before reinforcements arrived.

Mallet got to his knees and dislodged the last guard grappling him, throwing him a half a dozen feet back down the hallway, where he lay still. That was the last of them.

Mallet grinned, his face bright, his eyes shining. Then he saw the look on their faces, and he frowned. "What's wrong?"

Cael shook his head, "Forget it." There was no time to think about the violence. More Rothkin would come, and it would only get worse if he didn't hurry.

He walked to the strange wall with the Bystle Fruits growing in the shape of a tree. Time to see if Needle had been correct. He pressed his ring onto the wood.

A seam appeared and widened into an opening.

15th Day of Summer – 9:00 PM – The Moss Garden – 1 Hour Until the Full Moon

Cael entered the dark passageway beyond. There was a dim glow ahead. He walked for twenty feet until he came to a flight of stairs on the left. The glow came from above. He climbed up the stairs, followed by his companions.

The yellowy light grew brighter as they approached the top. Cael feared there would be more guards to make a final stand protecting the moss, but when they reached the garden, they were alone. The garden was a circular room maybe thirty or forty feet in diameter. It had a ceiling much higher than the hallways. Mallet, grinning ear to ear, stood up to his full height, his bald head brushing the inward growing branches where the glowing Bystle Fruits grew several times thicker than else-where. It was a real jungle of yellowy light up there.

Another hallway lay directly across from the one they en-tered, where there was another flight of stairs, this one leading up. Like the rest of the place, the room was formed directly from the smooth and polished wood of the trunk. Faces that seemed like some otherworldly type of ghosts stared at them from ev-ery polished wooden surface. A second glance confirmed that it was their own distorted reflections in the polished wood.

Cael suddenly felt a chill in the room, as if the temperature had dropped for a moment. Was there something here? Some-thing he was missing?

An altar of wood grew seamlessly up from the center of the room. On the altar grew a few tufts of bright-red, stringy moss. As he stared at the moss he felt his perceptions brighten, then dim. The moss seemed to waver, moving in a glowing, halluci-natory wave.

Cael felt a moment of elation. How difficult had it been to get to this point? From the moment Boxxaway's instructions had set them on the path to obtain this moss, it seemed like a flood of pain and suffering and setback. It felt like a veritable eternity of struggle just since they had entered the tree itself: sneaking, hiding, waiting... fighting. How long had they been in here on maximum alertness? Four hours? Five? And yet, here they were, finally. *And here was the moss.*

Brynn grabbed his arm, squeezed. He smiled at her. She understood.

He blinked, noting again how the moss wavered and flickered and seemed to move. The flow of Bystle Magic in the moss garden was intense. It seemed to be flowing directly at him, like a wind. And again, there was that strange sense of 'something' else; a darkness, a coolness. Something that set his nerves on edge.

Cael stepped closer to the altar into the buffeting flow of the emanating energetic wave. There was far less moss than Cael had expected. From the look of the crop, most of it had been picked away. Around the edges of the altar, the strands of the moss were broken away down to the nub. The growth was uneven and scraggly.

"So what now?" Mallet asked, reaching up to pick one of the fruits from an overhanging branch. "How do we darken this place?"

"Hold on!" Cael said quietly but sharply. "I don't think we should darken anything." Mallet pulled his hand back, letting go of the fruit.

"But the plan was to darken the moss and wait," Brynn said.

"That was Tharchelon's plan, not ours." Cael began to think about what he really wanted to do here.

"But what other options do we have?"

"Wait a minute," said Needle. "Cael might be right."

"What do you mean, 'might be'?" Brynn demanded. "We don't have much time. They are coming for us. We have to do something... now!"

"They'll come in strength," Mallet said, stamping the butt end of his glaive on the floor, making a thumping sound of wood on wood.

"Think about this," said Cael. "Tharchelon wants us to darken the place. Lower the barrier and let him back into the vale. Then what, just wait for him here? And when he gets here, do you really think he'll keep his promise and give us the moss and let us go?"

"I can hear sounds coming from below," Needle warned.

"So what other options do we have?" Brynn asked.

"Let's think this through," Cael said, circling around the moss altar. He allowed himself slip into a momentary meditative trance, considering the situation from all angles. As he did, he felt the flow of magic from the moss flowing outward in all directions, and then... he thought he could hear a faint hissing coming from nowhere and everywhere around him. Was the hiss connected to his chilled feeling?

"They are coming," Mallet said. He took up a position next to the entrance with his glaive at the ready. "I can hear them planning down there. We have no more than a minute or two."

"This is what we do," said Cael, coming to a conclusion. "We do *not* darken the room, we do *not* lower the barrier. Instead, we just take this moss, sneak out of here and find our way back to Demon's Bluff."

"But Tharchelon is out there," Mallet cautioned from the door. "And Wheizer."

"Exactly," Cael said. "And while we are getting the hells out, they will think we are still here inside. We stick to the wooded areas, head south out of the vale and hike to the edge of the escarpment. Find a way down. Meanwhile... we can start thinking of how to deal with... the full moon tonight."

"How do we get out of here?" Brynn shuddered, looking at her brother. "They're coming."

Cael grinned, feeling the flush of the wave of Bystle Magic buoying his spirits. "Where does the other stairway go?" he asked Needle.

"Up top... to the branches."

"I saw more of those flyers up there," said Cael. "When we were on the ground looking up at that archer shooting at us."

"You think you can fly us out of here on one of those things?" Brynn asked.

Cael wasn't at all sure, but he nodded anyway. The flyers would have to be their method of escape, as going back down wasn't going to be an option.

"What if Tharchelon or Wheizer come after us once we get out?" Brynn asked, doubtfully.

"They're going to do that anyway," said Cael. "This way, we leave them waiting at the barrier while we get a head start; maybe a big one if we can fly out. When the barrier doesn't drop, they will both assume we got captured or killed."

"It might be days before they even try to come looking for us..." Needle said, grinning.

"Here they come," Mallet said, repositioning himself by the entrance for the attack. "Whatever you are gonna do... do it now."

Cael stepped up to the moss altar with his dagger held firmly in his aching right hand. "I need a bag for this," he said.

Brynn fished a small leather pouch from her satchel. "Will this work?"

Cael used his dagger blade to shave the stringy red moss from the wood of the altar. It was tough and not easy to cut. He took the first handful of the harvested moss and stuffed it into the pouch. In short order, Cael had shorn about a third of the moss from the altar, when suddenly, the glowing fruits all blinked dark for a second.

"What the damnation was that about?" asked Mallet.

Cael had a sudden insight as to why, but there wasn't time for an answer. The sound of charging boots up the stairs reached them. Mallet turned and readied himself. Two Rothkin charged into the Moss Garden from the stairs. Mallet timed his blow expertly and swiped at them. His blade simultaneously eviscerated them both and pushed their bodies back down the stairs, obstructing the way and buying them precious seconds.

Cael paused, blade held in midair as the fruits blinked then stabilized and stayed lit. He resumed scraping the moss away from the wooden altar. The Bystle Fruits flickered again.

"Something is not right," said Brynn. "Is that happening because we are cutting away the moss?"

"I'm not positive," Cael said, continuing in earnest, but deep down he knew his cutting away the moss was absolutely causing the lights to flicker. The inward-growing Bystle Fruits were glowing based on the flow of the massive energy emanating from the moss... a flow that was diminishing as the harvest progressed.

He shoved the next bunch of cut moss into the sack.

Mallet suddenly swore savagely. Cael glanced up for only a moment and kept cutting. A Rothkin spear had pierced Mallet's thigh. He stumbled several steps back as two guards erupted through the entrance, spears held menacingly.

"Hurry!" Needle said, his voice inching up into a higher register. He had moved over to the base of the stairs at the opposite hallway.

A quarter of the moss remained un-harvested now as Cael continued to cut it away. The Bystle Fruits had begun to blink and flicker consistently. Additionally, it seemed the chill he felt earlier was getting stronger and the hissing... was it getting louder? Were there words in the hisses? Whispers?

"Hold them off, Mallet," Cael shouted, and continued to cut.

Mallet's glaive flashed in the yellowy light, parrying the spear thrusts of the growing number of Rothkin emerging from the stairs like angry ants boiling from an anthill.

Cael kept cutting. He became keenly aware that the flow of the strange Bystle Magic from the altar waned with every slice. What was once a wind of magical energy was now a mere breeze.

He kept cutting, realizing how powerful just this little bit of moss growing here had truly been. Until this moment, he had not fully comprehended the raw energy contained in these stringy red strands. The moss was indeed a powerful source of raw eldritch force . It was the source of magic for the whole vale. Tharchelon had said as much, but until Cael himself felt it, he did not truly understand it. What wizard wouldn't be tempted by this much power? With this moss, a wizard could cast unlimited spells, heedless of the cost he paid in months and years of his own life.

By providing a source of magic to the vale, the moss powered the glowing fruits and all else. From its origin at the moss, raw power flowed outward like a gale; so immensely powerful that it even drove away the *Arcanus Navitas* before it.

Cael glanced up again. The guards had begun to fan out slowly, in an effort to flank Mallet, who shuffled backward in an effort to keep a defensible position.

Just then, a commanding figure stepped to the top of the stairs. He had pitch black hair and wore dark robes. "Halt!" the newcomer commanded, holding both hands out, as if pleading for calm. His eyes flashed from Cael to the last remaining tuft of moss growing from the altar. His soldiers formed in a half circle around them.

Cael paused, his blade held inches from the last bit of moss. Nobody moved or spoke. Besides the black-haired leader, there were easily more than a dozen warriors armed with spears in the room. There were presumably more still in the stairwell. Mallet was wounded; blood soaked his pant leg. Cael supposed that Mallet could fight on with the wound, but even with him helping, he was sure they would all be overwhelmed or outright killed in short order.

Cael met the Rothkin leader's black, penetrating gaze directly. "You know what will happen if I cut this moss away, don't you?" Cael said. The Bystle Fruits flickered as if to punctuate his point.

The dark-robed Rothkin slowly stepped forward, his hands still held out. "My name is Nelcherath," he said in his thick, Rothkin accent. "Why don't we just calm down and see if we can come to an accord?"

"Nelcherath?" Needle asked from the base of the stairs behind Cael. "Tharchelon said you were a traitor."

Cael gritted his teeth, hoping Needle would just shut up. His big mouth had caused them enough problems already.

"Oh. And what else did that liar tell you?" Nelcherath responded, his eyes never leaving Cael's, though there was clearly a flicker of anger in his tone as he considered Tharchelon.

"He said he told you that we were coming to retrieve this moss," said Cael quickly to cut off Needle. "And that you decided you couldn't allow it. Was he lying about that?"

Nelcherath stared at Cael impassively for several seconds. "I presume he made a bargain with you," he said, his eyes drifting to the moss momentarily, then back to Cael.

"So it's haggling time," said Cael. "You want to offer something better than Tharchelon?" He tried to start gathering the oily Bystle Magic but found that with most of the moss gone there was very little to accumulate.

"Your lives and safe passage," Nelcharath offered. "You can keep what moss you have already gathered, but you must leave what remains."

"Tharchelon waits at the barrier even now," Cael said.

Nelcherath made no response. Cael searched his face but

it showed no hint of surprise. He either already knew it, or had surmised it.

"If he gets inside the barrier, it's all over for you," Needle said.

"That may be," Nelcherath said. "But not before you all die where you stand." He broke his steady gaze with Cael to glance down at the last bunch of moss.

Cael considered casting a spell, but the diminished flow of magic made it impossible.

He had to come up with something different and they might, indeed, have to make a bargain. He knew that Tharchelon was not to be trusted, and his instincts told him that neither was this Nelcherath an honorable person. He had to figure out another way out of this situation that did not depend on trusting a single Rothkin.

"I don't trust this guy," Needle said ironically.

And in that, Cael agreed completely. Then an idea came to him. He made a decision of what to do and didn't hesitate doing it. "Mallet, Brynn," he said, "move slowly over to Needle. Needle, take them and start making your way up the stairs out of here. Do not pause, do not think, just do it."

Nelcherath's eyes grew wide, but Cael gave a threatening look and adjusted his grip on the last tuft of moss. Nelcherath spread his hands out even farther to indicate that he wanted calm.

"But what are you going to do, Cael?" Brynn demanded.

"Brynn," Cael pleaded, "just do it."

Mallet backed to the stairs, signaling for Brynn to follow, which she did without further argument, though her green-eyed stare revealed she was not happy with this course of action.

With the anxious Rothkin looking on, Needle led Brynn and Mallet up the stairs from the Moss Garden. The sound of their footsteps faded away.

"So. You have decided to sacrifice yourself to save your friends," Nelcherath said after a long, tense minute.

"Not at all," Cael said. And with one quick cut he sheared the last tuft of moss from the surface of the wooden altar.

CHAPTER EIGHT
The Prisoner

"By death, we are born again. After birth, we die. After death, we are born. When will it ever end?"

- From the Writings of Xylex

15th Day of Summer - 6:45 AM – Tower of Rovule – Around 15 Hours Until the Full Moon

Elija Abel looked into the face of Cael and screamed.

From his first day of freedom after Tharchelon had rescued him, he had known to avoid the direct light of the sun. Mere daylight made him feel uncomfortable and detached, so he traveled in the shadows, mostly by night. The fog of that swamp had been a welcomed respite, as had been the rainy days.

Sunlight was dangerous. He did not know precisely what direct sunlight would do to him... but now, trapped under the massive stone, he was about to find out.

As the rays of the hateful morning sun fell upon him, he felt his sense of detachment grow. It grew and intensified until he felt something he had not felt in eons of undeath: pain. He felt as if he were being pulled apart. His vision flashed with the brightest of light and then the darkest of dark. The pain was exquisite. Perhaps he would finally be freed of his torment? Yet, a quiet simmering rage filled him. Xylex had sentenced him to 5000 years of hell... *for what?*

Oh, how he would have loved to have thwarted that wizard's scheme. He had thought about Xylex often. Xylex would have died not long after their last meeting those thousands of years ago. He wondered if Xylex, in whatever afterlife he found himself, was watching. Oh, how he would have loved to deal that one last measure of revenge!

But he let his anger go...

True death was black and sweet... after 5000 wretched years of suffering... boredom... it was all finally coming to a close. It did not matter that he failed in his revenge against the wizard's plot. He was free of his infernal prison. Peace at last...

Except...

A wrenching sensation... a heavy thud... a whirl of motion, a sense of creation... combining of bone and sinew...

He. Still. Lived. The pain from the sunlight lingered as he opened his eyes. The spirit shades of his descended sons milled about the altar where the moss grew. Blackness shone forth from the hanging orbs, casting their familiar gloom on the walls of his depressingly familiar prison dimension.

He was back in his shadowy torment. Alive still, in undeath; transported and reformed.

Quiet rage filled him.

Elija looked down. His sternum was caved in clear to his spine. Black ichor seeped in congealing rivulets from splits in his grayish skin. Organs peeked out here and there, forced out of his body by the crushing weight of the fallen obelisk. His monstrous right hand was mashed and nearly useless. His mutated appendage was a constant reminder of his hatred for Xylex. On that fateful day hundreds of generations ago, four of Xylex's *Balizars* had burrowed into the flesh of his forearm. Three of them had clawed their way out when the time was right so that he could leave them, as instructed, to serve as beacons. The fourth never emerged. He looked at his crushed mutant hand. The *Balizar* presumably had dissolved and become one with him. *Damn Xylex to the hottest layer of the infernal hells for eternity!*

He took a tentative, unbalanced step. He could move... stand. He considered another 5000 years trapped in this prison. He imagined eternity. It was hard to fathom but he was certain he had a better sense of it than anyone who had ever lived.

He thought back to that sunny day so many thousands of years ago, when he last spoke to Xylex. If he had only known then what price the wizard was exacting from him, he would have murdered him where he stood. Oh, that he could go back to that moment and redeem it!

He resigned himself. His spirit sons settled like leaves in autumn. How had his prey managed to topple that obelisk onto him? They somehow knew to expose him to the sun. Was it dumb luck? Perhaps fate conspired with them to return him to this hateful place. His anger fermented.

15th Day of Summer - 9:00 PM – The Alternate Moss Dimension – 1 Hour to the Full Moon

In this place, time lost its meaning. Elija's only true measure of time was the life span of his sons. Each time one died, his tortured spirit was drawn by the accursed moss, arriving in this place. Each arrival signaled the passing of yet another generation.

He thought again of the day that Tharchelon had freed him; outside this prison in the Moss Garden at last. He had looked directly at the accursed stuff and thought back to the first and only time he had ever tasted it. It was just another in a long series of mistakes he'd made. It was a mistake he knew he would never make again. Besides, in undeath he could see and hear, but smell taste and touch had abandoned him. With those senses gone, he had lost all taste for physical passions, though his anger and hatred remained in full force. He had resisted the temptation and, without a second look, walked out of the Moss Garden. He thought he would never see this place again, but fate had stabbed him in the back once more.

Elija did not know how long he had been back in this prison, but it seemed to him a very short time. Something was changing. The shades of his sons grew suddenly agitated. He could sense their fear... their rage.

He turned his gaze to the altar and the moss that grew upon it. Was it diminished? Was Tharchelon back picking away at it once more?

No. A large section of it was missing from the altar. What was happening?

It could mean only one thing: his failure was complete.

Cael and his cohorts had arrived. They were in the Moss Garden... harvesting the moss at this very moment.

Was that a voice he heard? *"Something...right..."*

The gloom from the fruits flickered to a harsh yellow for a moment.

Could he see movement near the altar... a movement not made by his sons? No... it was gone. Had he imagined it?

No... the movement was there again.

Another tuft of moss faded from the altar. The darkness flashed to yellow light and back again.

"Hurry!" He heard it distinctly this time. He was sure it was one of the four.

Something *was* happening. The kids were harvesting the moss, but here, on the other side, it caused some disturbance... some change.

He knew every crag and cranny in this place. He knew the shape of the altar, the grain pattern of every square inch of the gray, monotone wood. He could also feel the change in the energy that the moss exuded. It was all changing. Subtly, slowly, but changing. The gloom from the fruits flickered yellow again.

As he looked around, the first significant thing he noticed were the walls of his prison. Directly across from each other, patches of lighter wood appeared. They began to form into a growing concavity that hollowed out into halls. He knew them both from when Tharchelon had first freed him from this prison. Were the separate dimensions at this place growing closer together? As the energy of the moss waned, the integrity of *this* place was waning with it.

He looked back to the altar. He could see them now. They seemed distant and indistinct but he could see the barest outlines of the four children. One stood by each hallway, and two by the altar.

"Hold them off!" he heard. Yes! He was correct. That was the voice of the one called Cael.

The shades were howling now. They too could feel the moss being cut away. The pathetic source of their fascination and their torment was being reaped.

Elija sensed others... more creatures were coming into the Moss Garden.

"...*liar tell you...*" He discerned another voice speaking. Rothkin? Perhaps Tharchelon himself? He strained to see through the veil between dimensions, but it was still unclear.

Three of the forms suddenly headed to the hallway behind the altar. They were large, one was huge. The boy he had fought in the swamp, he surmised, with his damnable dog.

"*Just do it,*" he heard the words barely. The three forms disappeared and fled up the stairs. One still stood by the altar. He felt certain it was Cael.

The shapes he saw were indistinct and the distant voices continued to drift across to him. Only fragments of words now reached him. The shades of his sons still howled. He calmed them down, commanding them to stillness so he could listen. They did not obey. They were restless and angry; their precious moss was almost gone.

Then... something momentous occurred. The phrase "*not at all*" drifted across from the other side, followed by a long moment of haunted anticipation...what was happening?

The last bunch of moss on the altar vanished. He felt a massive wobble as if a shockwave had pulsed past him.

His consciousness spun. Soundless fury whirled around him. His existence seemed to descend into an unending, spiraling, empty void... then calm. The dark fruits flickered and flared. The gloom of this place vanished, replaced by a steady, yellowy glow.

Everything went silent and still, even the shadows of his sons.

Elija could see more plainly now into the Moss Garden on the other side. It was like looking at fish through the ripples of a fast-moving brook. It was shifting and distorted, but he could see. It was dark there--very dark. But he could see Cael crouched down behind the altar. The moss was entirely harvested. Cael was stuffing the last tuft into a sack.

I should have killed him from the start, he thought. When he first met the boy, he destroyed the orb when he should have killed him instead. He felt a small twitch of emotion regarding his mistake. Such mistakes had led him to countless lifetimes of torment.

It was the hated orbs that made him do it; the *Balizars* that had crawled onto his hand and burrowed painfully into his flesh. Just seeing the little orb rolling around in Cael's palm had blinded him. He should have killed Cael, but all he wanted to do was destroy the orb. He looked down at his mangled, deformed hand. His entire life was a series of mistakes. What he needed was redemption.

The assembled spirits of his sons rose from their somnolence and began to rage, avalanching over Cael. They could sense the harvested moss he carried with him. Perhaps the veil between them was so thin that he could find a way to escape? He took a step toward Cael and reached out with his mangled right hand, his deformed fingers grasping. Was he still trapped in this prison, or was he free? He needed confirmation.

As he feared, his fingers passed right through Cael. This place was changed, expanded, but it was still intact. However, the veil between the two dimensions *was* growing thinner.

He turned his attention back to the newly-formed hallway, walking over to it. Would he be able to step through? A sudden hope gripped him. Maybe he would be able to escape this place.

He took a tentative step onto the bottom stair and slowly began to climb. Perhaps he would get his opportunity for redemption after all...

CHAPTER NINE
Keys to Ascension

"We have no need for allies when fear is on our side."

- Xylex

15th Day of Summer - 9:00 PM – Among the Ancients – 1 Hour Until the Full Moon

Cael heard Nelcherath scream as the bystle fruits gave one last dying pulse, a single heartbeat, the light turning from yellow to red to deep blue, and then fading with tracers of smeared purple ... into a void went the coruscating lucence.

Time seemed to stand still as Cael and every Rothkin inside the hollowed out tree were plunged into thick, impenetrable darkness. The dark came as no surprise to him but its suddenness and depth filled him with a choking fear that can only come with being completely blind. His remaining senses fought to recalibrate, unsure of which should take on the sensory burden now that his eyes were left obsolete. As his senses warred, the memory of his mother's murder suddenly surfaced in his consciousness. The thick darkness, combined with the horrible memory, triggered a feeling of emptiness that made the hair on the back of his neck stand on end. Or was there something more?

His time was short; he had to get out of here quickly. With the last of the moss cut away, he had felt certain that the light from the fruits would fail. His reasoned calculation was that the barrier keeping Tharchelon out of the vale would fail with it. The big question was, would Nelcherath make the same calculation? His scream seemed an encouraging sign that he, too, understood.

Cael shoved the last clump of moss into the bag and hunkered low behind the altar. Out of the frozen blackness came the wailing sound of Rothkin chaos, just as he had hoped. He could feel the claustrophobic terror of the Rothkin as they fumbled and groped about. He had a sudden insight; they had never been without the warm glow of the bystle fruit inside this ancient tree. Panicked shouts of retreat barely echoed over terrified screams. Was Nelcherath issuing the commands? The Rothkin confusion bore testimony that his moment for escape was at hand.

Before he shaved away the last of the moss, he'd formed a mental picture of where the stairs were. He took a breath in preparation to dash over to the stairwell when he suddenly felt the imminent proximity of a host of unholy horrors so ancient and powerful as to make everything he had experienced thus far in life seem childish by comparison. A symphony of hissing whispers erupted around him as if an innumerable assemblage cried out in simultaneous rage. Among the jumble of hissing voices he could barely make out a few words... words that filled him with dread: *usurper... thief... cur... lecherous... murder.* The memories of his parent's murders, the cold dread of the shrine, even the dead eyes of Elija Abel paled in comparison to the terror building in him. His chest constricted and he felt like his ribs were being slowly pressed together.

Hearing was bad enough, but what was much worse, he could *feel* the presence of the multitude of malevolent beings bent on his utter destruction. Cael tried desperately to move but mindless fear overwhelmed him. Some unnatural malignancy infected this place; let loose upon him, he was certain, as a consequence of harvesting the moss. He had expected the darkness. But what he hadn't expected was revelation that something best left trapped had been let loose. Panic paralyzed him.

Cael could not breathe. Would he black out here? Would he be consumed by whatever nefarious swarm had got ahold of him?

He forced himself to think of anything but the evil that possessed him. His mind cast about in desperation for a redeeming thought to hold on to, and settled on a memory still fresh and unforgettable: his mother's face. He thought of her smile, her kind brown eyes, twinkling with tears, sweat glistening on her brow as she held him the one and only time.

He suddenly released his held breath with a moan and gained control of his senses for the briefest of moments. The hissing horde still raged about him... *bastard... kill.... molester... treachery... eviscerate,* but he was able to summon the strength to act by sheer force of his will.

He breathed in and lunged, crawling on all fours (still holding his dagger in his wounded right hand) toward where he knew the exit was. The strain of keeping a grip on the dagger and putting weight on his knuckles sent jags of pain shooting up his entire arm, but he had no choice but to press forward.

As he scampered, something suddenly groped his left ankle. His immediate thought was that the sinister force was closing in on him, but he quickly realized it must be one of the Rothkin warriors. A hand grasped at the straps of his boots then another hand latched on, pulling him back. He looked back, but could see nothing in the pressing blackness.

Cael kicked furiously to shake the halfling loose, but the little bastard was clamped on tightly, trying to go hand over hand up his leg. His blow glanced off. He kicked again and this time, whether out of luck or desperation, his foot connected and he felt, more than heard, a meaty crunch. The Rothkin's grip loosened momentarily and a sudden screech punctuated the room. The sound was one of surprised pain gurgling through something wet. Cael imagined the unseen Rothkin's bloody nose smeared across his diminutive face as he surged in the direction of what he hoped was the stairwell.

He had a clear mental image of where those stairs were, but, whether due to the strange, haunting horrors or the distraction of the Rothkin attacking him, he misjudged and smashed his head straight into a wall. The impact sent an intense, dizzying shock through his skull. Phantom stars popped in his vision and a sharp pain on the top of his head made his eyes water instantly.

To make matters worse, his dogged pursuer re-established his grip on Cael's boot. Cael felt himself being dragged inexorably back into the center of the Moss Garden.

The thought of being captured, or worse, being taken back to the malevolent force that had assailed him, caused a worming terror to crawl its way up his throat and spew forth as a horrified scream. He flailed blindly for something to hold onto and banged his hand on the floor. Pain cascaded up his arm.

The pain was a blessing. He suddenly remembered he was holding the dagger. He swung blindly where he thought his attacker was, but missed completely. His attacker, sensing the danger, lunged forward. Fingers, impossibly strong for their child-like size, grabbed at Cael's hair and face, desperately seeking to gouge his eyes. The Rothkin had made a mistake going for his eyes instead of his hands. Cael shook his head back and forth violently to avoid the probing fingers, and with his right hand free, he now knew the exact location of his attacker. He swung his arm up and jammed the dagger between the ribs of his opponent, sinking it to the hilt, warm sticky blood seeping across his hand and wrist.

His foe grunted and rolled off him to the left as Cael yanked the knife out of the slack body. Visions of his mother's bloody death at the point of the same blade intruded, but he forced them from his mind.

Cael clutched the dagger to his chest with both hands and breathed deeply, mentally taking inventory of his own body as he lay there. The angry hissing found him again, indistinct angry whispers of hatred emanating all around him. Another vomit of terror rose up his throat, almost causing him to scream again. Discernable words once again seeped from the jumbled whispers into his consciousness: *"pig... moss.... defiler... kill."* Cael felt as if his sanity would fail, leaving him gibbering in utter madness.

He wanted to crawl out of his own skin, but found the will to flip himself over and scramble back toward where he hoped the stairs were. He felt around hysterically when his hand landed on a solid step. He had just missed the steps by inches earlier, smashing his head into the wall.

He dove forward once again and shot up and onto the stairs. He raced up the stairway on all fours in the pitch blackness. He paid no heed to anything behind him, only focused on going up and out as fast as he could move.

Was he being chased? He doubted the Rothkin were after him. Nelcherath knew the score; the barrier was down and Tharchelon was coming.

Even if the Rothkin were after him, he much preferred them to the malign presence that had assaulted him. Something unnatural and evil, but no less real, and much more terrifying than the Rothkin was down there. He wanted no more to do with it.

"Brynn! Mallet!" he hissed as he climbed. He felt a tickling sensation on the left side of his neck. He touched it and felt a slick wetness.

A faint whitish blue light eventually became visible from above. Cael could see that the straight stairs above him began to curve into a spiral. Brynn must have activated her stone sigil. He kept going. *Up and out.* That was all he could think, not even noticing that his left hand was covered in blood from where he had touched his neck, where it poured copiously from the head wound he had given himself when he crashed into the wall.

The ambient light grew brighter as he climbed and he finally felt safe enough to risk one look back into the engulfing darkness. His heart seized momentarily as he did so, prepared to witness something anciently vile and timelessly evil. But all he saw was darkness.

The spiral stairway ascended for what seemed forever. Cael managed to stay sufficiently ahead of whatever evil he was convinced was pursuing him. He couldn't help but wonder... had the Rothkin been as tormented by whatever malign force was down there? He was breathing hard from his climb but he couldn't hear sounds from below. Had the Rothkin retreated to defend against Tharchelon's attack as he hoped? Or had they been killed by the evil force that had assailed him? Cael imagined the corpses of dead Rothkin, lifeless eyes still open, fear still etched on their faces. The thought gave him a shiver. The consequence of taking the last bunch of moss might have been far worse than he could have ever imagined. He redoubled his efforts to climb. *Up and out.*

Then he heard it. A host of whispers from below him, almost indiscernible... and yet he did discern some words... *"maggot... rend... whore."*

Despite the thick air, exhaustion and his near-hysterical emotions, he managed to keep going and finally arrived at a landing, a wide hallway about ten feet long, dead-ending in a blank wooden wall. His three companions stood with their backs to him. Mallet was chopping furiously at a discolored section of the wall with his glaive, sending woodchips flying. A bloody bandage was tied around his thigh.

Brynn and Needle heard him over Mallet's noise and turned. She broke into a relieved smile, the glowing piece of rock cupped in her palm. As Cael drew closer, Brynn's smile faded, her eyes widened and her jaw dropped.

"It looks worse than it is," Cael said. "It's just a cut on my scalp." He realized he needed to be calm or everyone would panic. He was on the verge of panic himself.

"This whole thing is way worse than we thought it, isn't it?" Needle asked, his face curiously pale in the glow of Brynn's light.

The indistinct hissing noise grew louder as it approached up the stairs. Cael fought back a sense of dread. Would Needle and Brynn be able to hear it over the sound of Mallet's chopping? For the moment, they seemed not to notice. He steadied himself and desperately tried to control his breathing. He suddenly thought of the *Arcanus Navitas*. Perhaps with the magic of the moss gone, it would return?

If there was any thought that could have pushed Cael over the edge into full blown panic, it was what he discovered next. He reached for the *Arcanus Navitas,* but it was utterly absent. Only the barest ripple of the slippery magic remained, ebbing even as he sensed it. He felt helpless. Since his grandfather had taught him to sense the *Arcanus Navitas*, Cael had never experienced such a dearth of magic.

"Taste it."

Cael whirled, startling both Brynn and Needle.

"Did you hear that?" Cael asked. A disembodied voice, gravelly and of low tone, had spoken right into his ear. It was not at all like the many whispers. Had he imagined it?

"Hear what?" Needle said as Mallet continued chopping away.

"Taste it."

Cael whirled again and thought he caught a shadowy glimpse of gray and black. But then it was gone.

"What the abyss is that?" Needle asked nervously, stepping over to the edge of the landing. "Can you hear that? It sounds like a hissing noise." He looked down the stairwell and turned back toward them, his eyes wide, mouth agape.

Faint words could be heard through a tornado of hisses *"ravage... plunderer... bastard... kill."*

Brynn took several steps backward in a rush, bumping into Mallet. "What's going on, Cael?" she said, her every word rooted in a terror so intense that her eyes began to water. Needle stood stock still, a look of horror on his face.

Mallet, oblivious, readjusted himself and resumed hacking away at the wood with renewed fury.

A litany of near faint shadows surged over the edge of the landing, undulating toward them, hissing as they moved. Brynn looked as if she desperately wanted to scream but the sound was paralyzed in her chest.

The air was getting colder, and Cael's breathing became shallower. Then he heard the raspy voice again: *"Save them. Use the moss and save them."*

Cael fumbled in his pockets, his hand coming to rest on the pouch of moss he had tucked away. There was no magic here... except for the moss. What avail was it to anyone if they died here at the hands of this shadowy swarm?

"Just one taste can save them."

The hissing shadows moved closer and Mallet finally saw and heard. *"Rip... thief... torment... death..."* The glaive slipped free from his hands, his tanned face gone pale.

"Cael!" Brynn urged, grabbing his arm. "The ring! Use the

ring to open the door!"

Of course! Cael nodded dumbly, fished out the ring. He slipped it onto his little finger as he shuffled past Brynn and Mallet in the confined hallway. He touched it to the wall where Mallet had been chopping.

Cael pushed the ring harder into the wood wall, but nothing happened. Desperate hopelessness gripped him. They would all die here. Then... the faintest of seams formed vertically on the wall. The seam grew deeper ever so slowly and the portal began to creak open until it lost momentum and stopped. Only the faintest light from outside shone through.

"Why isn't it working?" Needle demanded hysterically.

Cael knew the answer. The moss had been the source of power and now that power was gone. "Because there is no more magic left to make it work."

They were trapped. The cold insidious shadows frothed about them, each whispered word plucked from the maelstrom of hisses more frightening than the last. "*Hate... gnaw... vile... slaughter...*"

"*Taste it,*" soothed the raspy voice in his ear.

Cael reached into his pocket again and wormed his fingers into the drawstring opening of the pouch.

"*You can save them.*"

He touched the moss, and felt a slightly sticky strand between his thumb and middle finger.

Am I evil?

He withdrew his fingers and shoved the bag of moss deep into his pocket. *No... I... Will... Not!*

Mallet suddenly retrieved his glaive and shoved him aside. He rammed the blade into the seam, levering it open. To Cael's amazement, the wood responded to the force and opened a little more. Mallet jammed his fingers through the widened gap and began to pull it apart. Cael could see the huge muscles in Mallet's arms and neck strain and bulge against the slightly yielding wood. Amazingly, he was able to slowly widen the gap. His glaive fell free and clattered to the floor. Needle picked it up. Mallet had a gap wide enough that he could angle his shoulder against one side of the gap, and push on the other side with his mighty arms. After another moment, he had wedged himself in the gap with the knee on his good leg also pushing for leverage. A broad branch topped with a wooden catwalk was visible outside the door.

A waft of fresh air hit them... Cael sucked it in between his teeth and filled his lungs to the brim. Damnation! It was the sweetest air he had ever tasted. And in that moment, his despair ebbed.

"Needle," he said.

Needle did not need to be told twice. He tossed the glaive out onto the catwalk and dove through the space under Mallet's straining thigh.

Mallet held the gap open wide enough for Brynn and then Cael to pass through.

Mallet did not move immediately. He was staring back the way they had come. Cael thought he might have to grab the boy and pull, but then Mallet grunted and shoved himself out onto the catwalk. His face was pale and uncomprehending as the gap snapped shut.

CHAPTER TEN
Vengeance: The Pact

"I have often pondered the motives of those who flocked to the cult's banner. Some are driven by lust for power or wealth, which is easy enough to understand. But others are driven by emotions devoid of logic or reason. Many are possessed of an unquenchable thirst for revenge against a society they perceive as having wronged them in some incomprehensible way."

- Gadrax Von Torinovo

15th Day of Summer - 9:30 PM – Half an hour Until the Full Moon

Elija stood watching as the portal snapped shut after the enormous boy slipped out. He had tried desperately to push past through the opening as the children wormed their way out of the tree, but to no avail.

His prison had morphed and enlarged itself in the wake of the moss being harvested, but a prison it remained. He gazed at the shades of his sons. Some remained at the landing with him, frantically probing the new walls of their shadowy dimension, desperate to follow the intruder who had stolen their dearest moss. Others had fled back down the stairs, vainly hoping to find a remnant upon the altar to give them comfort.

Not only was he unable to escape, but he had also failed to prevent the four rotten teenagers from escaping. He had used the only influence he could wield, speaking across the thin dimensional barrier directly into the boy Cael's ear--tempting him. Every indication was that the boy had heard him and given weight to his words, but in the end he did not succumb. But perhaps there was still hope that the boy would capitulate and addict himself. He would destroy the moss and himself in the process. There was a weakness in the boy, he was certain of it. The boy would wilt if enough pressure came upon him.

Elija felt despondent. Even if the boy did give in to temptation, how would he ever know? It would not be as satisfying as hunting him down and slowly choking the life from him. Elija imagined setting the moss aflame on Cael's newly-dead corpse as Xylex watched on in despair.

Elija smiled. He made a pact with himself: *he would have his vengeance no matter the cost, no matter the wait.* In time, this shadow dimension must weaken further. Eventually he would find a way out and when he did, *he would have his redemption.* He had not seen the last of the boy Cael or his friends. He smiled again.

CHAPTER ELEVEN
Close to the Edge

"Many days' journey west of Taglyon, along the southern coast, there is a mountainous area that has come to be known as the 'Westcliffs'. There, sheer rock walls, risen to dizzying heights, meet the sea. In that place where the fabled Rocs nest, one can only imagine the view from atop the precipice looking down the sheer drop to the pounding surf far below."

-Excerpted from *"The Southern Sea"* by Puppus Chugg, Taglyon Loremaster of Flora & Fauna

15th Day of Summer - 9:30 PM – Bystle Tree Branches – Half an Hour to the Full Moon

Cael's sense of panic quickly ebbed as he emerged from the tree. He was relieved to see that the golden, brilliant light of the setting sun still painted the woods. The cloudy sky on the western horizon was aflame with reds, oranges and purples. No full moon. Not yet. The last thing he needed now was Mallet to emerge into the light of a full moon and turn into a wererat.

Cael turned quickly and soaked up his surroundings. Needle was crouched next to him doing the same. The sun had set but it was still quite light out. A warm summer breeze swirled around them. From his vantage, he could see that most of the giant branches jutting from the massive tree were topped with a network of ten-foot-wide catwalks. Webbed between the catwalks were wooden bridges that encircled the mighty trunk in free-floating concentric rings. The catwalk they occupied was built onto the lowest level of branches encircling the enormous trunk. It was from this level that they had been fired upon by the archer when they were at the base of the tree. It had to be at least 300 feet straight down. Above them were more levels of branches with networks of platforms, catwalks, bridges and ladders. Each level, including their own, was abuzz with Rothkin activity. However, their presence was still unnoticed.

Looking down, Cael saw Tharchelon's forces in the distance, charging toward the tree. The harvesting of the moss had indeed lowered the barrier. The battle between the two Rothkin factions would begin to rage in mere moments.

"What in the abyss was that in there?" Needle hissed, looking back at the seam in the wood from which they had emerged.

"I think something got let loose when I cut the last piece of Moss," Cael confessed.

"Loose? What?" Brynn whispered as she scanned the branches around them.

"I don't know for sure," said Cael in a low voice. "But I'm glad as hells to be out of there. I've never been more scared."

"We heard a scream, we thought you were dead," Brynn whispered.

"We have other things to worry about now," Cael said. "We have to find a way down. We won't stay unnoticed for much longer."

Suddenly the warm breeze turned cooler, sending a shiver through him. The terrifying memory of the whispers intruded again. Boxxaway liked to tell scary stories and more than once, Cael had delightfully shivered in his bed, blankets pulled up tight to his chin, while his grandfather gleefully scared the sand out of him by candlelight. But that had been 'fun' fear, stories of thumb collectors, risen mummies and Agrabi shamans who kidnapped Buerdeleise children and spirited them away to the deep desert. The fear from the whispers was something else entirely; the kind of primal terror that threatened to push you past the brink of sanity to drown in your own panic.

As Cael wrestled with the memory of the haunting fear, he could hear muffled orders being shouted, distant screams as warriors died in battle and the raucous clatter of clashing weapons. A sizzling thunderclap from a Rothkin lightning crossbow snapped him back to the moment. It was a sound he knew well. He caught sight of two of the strange flying machines dropping into his field of vision. Each flyer was manned by a pilot and a gunner, like the one they had faced earlier. With a high-pitched whirring sound, they dove down with incredible speed at Tharchelon's forces. Both flyers had a glowing fruit impaled upon a spike at the rear of the machine.

Other than these fruits, however, the rest of the fruits growing throughout the massive canopy around him were not glowing at all. Cael guessed the fruits still on the tree had lost all their magic, while the fruits that had been picked previously still retained their power. The harvested, glowing Bystle Fruits were little reservoirs of magic, which would seem to give Nelcherath's side an advantage since Tharchelon's forces wouldn't have any of the fleshy glowing fruits, much less the flying machines.

The flyers patrolled at the limit of Tharchelon's arrow fire, periodically firing lightning bolts from the mounted crossbows. Some bolts missed their targets, impacting the ground with a flash of light and smoking spray of charred earth. Some found their targets and Cael watched as one bolt hit at the front of a charging formation, killing several of Tharchelon's soldiers.

Tharchelon's forces carried what looked like large shields, struggling to maintain some semblance of formation as they rushed in. Several dozen of Tharchelon's archers followed behind, firing arrows in long arcs to keep the flyers at bay.

In the tree several dozen Rothkin were out on the catwalks, firing arrows down at the onrushing invaders. Teams of Rothkin stationed on platforms interspersed throughout the branches fired mounted ballistae that hurled javelins an impressive distance. Very few arrows or javelins found their mark. The diminishing light made for difficult shooting, and the invaders were bunched together, huddled under upturned shields.

Cael looked around. All the Rothkin were focused on the battle shaping up on the ground below. Thankfully, the four of them continued to remain unnoticed in the chaos... for the moment.

Cael scanned around for a means of escape and found what he was looking for. About fifty feet away, there was a platform where one of the strange flying machines was perched. Upon its spike was impaled a large, glowing Bystle Fruit. Two Rothkin had just reached it and were busily preparing it.

To reach the flyer, they'd have to abandon their relative seclusion and cross a suspended bridge to a walkway on an entirely different branch. All the Rothkin had their attention directed outward to the battle, not inward to the trunk of the tree where they were now. If there was a time to try... this was it.

"Follow me," Cael hissed, making the decision for everyone. He didn't have time to consult them; that flyer would launch and be gone if they didn't hurry. He began creeping along the catwalk.

"Cael, are you crazy?" Brynn whispered. "We'll be seen!"

Cael didn't answer. He headed for the suspended bridge to cross to the next branch over. The others followed cautiously, though he could feel Brynn's eyes burning a hole in his back.

As he moved, he kept an eye on the action below. Countless dozens of Nelcherath's warriors emerged from their hiding places among the exposed roots of the tree below them. Nelcherath's forces began to form up to meet the oncoming charge from Tharchelon's army. A horn blew a long lingering note in the distance and the invaders began to charge with a terrifying yell. Even from the high vantage, Cael could sense that Tharchelon's troops were much more motivated than those defending the mammoth tree.

As Cael trotted toward the flyer, he instinctively reached out to gather magic, but of course there was far too little of it to bother. The *Arcanus Navitas* was still absent, and the alien Bystle Magic was barely detectable.

What about the moss?

He banished the thought. Outside in the fresh air, it was easier to do.

He stopped short on the catwalk. Needle ran into the back of him. "We have to get them out of there," Cael whispered, pointing to the two Rothkin who had climbed into the flyer and were busily strapping themselves in.

"You mean to fly us out of here?" Brynn asked, a desperate look on her face as she peered over the edge at the ground hundreds of feet below.

"Mallet. Needle," Cael whispered pointing at the two Rothkin. Mallet nodded and pushed past, spinning the haft of his glaive expertly. Needle gave Cael a dark look, but followed close behind.

"Do you know how to fly one of those things?" Brynn asked.

"I'll figure it out," Cael said with a confidence meant to mask his doubts.

Cael looked down. He noticed Tharchelon among a group of Rothkin hanging far back behind the main fighting. The king was much larger than most of his compatriots. Several adjutants were with him as he surveyed the battle.

Just then, Mallet reached the platform. With a mighty lunge, he thrust the butt of his glaive, instantly knocking the pilot unconscious.

The gunner cried out loudly in surprise and fumbled furiously with his crossbow, but Mallet pulled his glaive back and swung the butt end toward the little Rothkin in a single fluid motion, impacting his head with a sickening crack. The gunner dropped limp in his straps.

Cael marveled at Mallet's fluid puissance. His quick thinking had gained them some critical seconds.

In a flash, Needle was on the pilot, slicing at the leather straps that held his limp body. He cut the pilot free and, struggling with visible effort, he unceremoniously rolled the limp form onto the platform.

Cael felt Brynn touch his shoulder. He turned his head to look at her. She was staring in horror as her brother cut the gunner free of his straps and dumped him in a similar fashion.

An arrow whizzed past Cael and another thudded into the branch just below the platform where they stood. The gunner's cry of warning had been heard. A gang of Rothkin archers across the way abandoned firing at the battle below in favor of firing at them. Fortunately, their arrows needed arc to reach them and the overhanging canopy of thick leaves interfered with most of the shots. The Rothkin realized the problem instantly and began racing toward them along the catwalks.

Cael didn't hesitate. He leaped into the front of the flyer. His hand slid on the slick, blood-covered seat and he sat down in the smear he had just created. The iron smell of blood infiltrated Cael's nostrils. He wiped his bloody hand on his pant leg as he squeezed into the pilot's perch.

He had no idea what to expect by way of controls, but what he found petrified him: There were none! He felt about the enclosure in desperation hoping to find some manner of tiller or lever to fly this machine. Arrows sliced through the air around them. Some of the archers had paused to fire, while the rest continued running toward them at full speed along the web of catwalks and bridges. Cael knew they had but seconds.

The machine suddenly rocked back and forth as Brynn and Needle scrambled aboard. Then it heaved violently forward as Mallet leapt on. For one horrifying moment, Cael thought that Mallet's momentum would drive the machine over the front edge of the platform. He instinctively reached forward and grabbed hold of a wooden bar in front of him. In that instant he understood.

This flying machine was a magical device not unlike Boxxaway's flying carpet, or the lifts on the cliff back in Demon's Bluff. This flyer derived power from the magical glowing fruit impaled on the spike by the gunner's perch.

Arrows struck the platform around them. The shouting Rothkin were firing at them in earnest, and drawing the attention of other Rothkin who also began to close in. Brynn cried out in pain, but Cael didn't have time to turn his attention away from the flyer.

He closed his eyes and plugged himself into the magic coursing through the flyer. It was the same sort of oily, alien magic that flowed from the moss, so very unlike the familiar *Arcanus Navitas*. But Cael understood this magic now... somewhat, at least. It flowed from the impaled fruit into the flying machine. In the same way that old wizards who operated the lifts back in Demon's Bluff were able to operate them without expending their own life force, Cael could tap into the magic inside the flyer to operate it.

Cael willed the machine forward, using the same technique that Boxxaway had taught him to form magic in his mind into a usable force. He pushed down and back with his mind. He was not at all surprised when the flyer began to scrape forward across the platform. Normally, Cael would have stopped to consider his plan more carefully, but there was no time for that. The Rothkin arrows continued to whiz about them.

Cael pushed down and back with a mighty heave and the flyer lurched forward off the edge of the platform.

To Cael's complete dismay, they plummeted straight down.

CHAPTER TWELVE
The Battle of Bystle Vale

"One drawback with training generals in battle command is that it stifles their ability to think creatively. They rely too much on their training and not enough on their wits. The key to victory has never been found in the size of one's army. The key to victory always lies in innovative tactics and strategy."

- Alliance Field Marshall, Asher Spirovenko

15th Day of Summer – 8:30 PM – Outside the Barrier – 90 Minutes to the Full Moon

Tharchelon sat with his back against the damnable barrier. Flashbacks of the day he had been kicked out of the vale flickered momentarily through his mind. *Revenge would be sweet. Oh, Nelcherath... Oh, Ockler...*

But not as sweet as a pinch of the moss... no... that would be sweeter even than revenge.

He shivered, despite the warmth on his face from the sun, which now touched the western horizon. He drew his knees up to his chest as he replayed his plan again in his mind. If all went according to plan, then Cael and the others should be in the tree by now; maybe even in the Moss Garden itself, waiting for night to come.

"We are making the final preparations to the new equipment, my King," Rathenel said, his approach casting a shadow over Tharchelon.

"The new shields ready?" Tharchelon asked.

"We are ahead of schedule. The last of the hides arrived from the camp a few hours ago. Most of the shields are built and only a few remain unfinished."

Tharchelon shaded his eyes with his hand. The warriors of his ragtag force were milling about busily. Mostly they were engaged in putting the final touches on the array of mismatched large shields made of hide, bark or freshly hewn shingles. Each stood much taller and wider than an average Rothkin warrior. The shields had been his idea. If the barrier came down and Tharchelon's forces invaded, Nelcherath would be forced to rely heavily on his archers firing from the branches of the Bystle Tree.

Then there was the problem of the flyers. Surprise was vital as the new shields would be scant defense against a lightning bolt.

Frankly, he'd surprised himself coming up with the shield strategy. His mind was clouded, troubled. Without the clarity the Bystle Moss afforded him, it was very hard to concentrate. Indeed, he had thought himself incapable of such clear thinking without a taste of moss to help. Even now, his yearning for such a taste made it difficult to focus on any thought without interruption. A taste would settle his nerves... help him think clearly... make his worries fade.

His worries... his worries were legion! So much could go wrong with his plan. Chief among his concerns were the miserable outlanders. Would they be able to sneak through the tree and get to the Moss Garden undetected? If indeed they made it, would they follow through and lower the barrier as instructed? He had thought on that very question long and hard. *Yes*, he'd concluded. They would do exactly as he had commanded them. After all, didn't he hold captive the mouthy one as insurance? They had no choice. His worry was that proper motivation simply did nothing to guarantee them safe passage into the Moss Garden. *Damn hells, if they don't get that far, all is lost.* He felt a sudden welling of despair, but quickly forced the doubts from his mind.

He looked again toward the setting sun. He would know soon enough. If the barrier was going to fall, it would happen in the next few hours. He rubbed his tongue against the roof of his mouth expectantly. The wait of a few short hours seemed an eternity of torture.

He cursed himself for his predicament. He thought back to that moment when he'd first tasted the infernal stuff. If he could undo that moment, he would. A thousand times he would!

That first taste had ultimately cost him everything. Here he sat, back against the invisible barrier that exiled him from his own kingdom. He was utterly helpless... at the mercy of outlander children for any hope of reclaiming his throne. He looked again at his meager army. Assuming that the three succeeded and the barrier came down, it then fell to these few pathetic followers. His hopes then rested upon them for regaining all that he had lost... all that the accursed moss had cost him... all that it had cost his people. He cursed himself again.

He stared skyward. Streaks of color from the setting sun infused the growing cloud cover. How long had it been since he last tasted the moss? Had it been almost a week? His sense for the passage of time felt muddled... more than a week? Regardless, hadn't he survived without the moss, lo these many days? Wasn't he stronger than it was? He was King of the Bystle Vale, after all; subject to the will of no one... no thing. Yet, despite his noble lineage and his kingly birthright, he was powerless; utterly at the mercy of whim and circumstance. *He desperately needed control.* If nothing else, he needed to *feel* as if he were in control. He felt a tear welling at the corner of his eye.

"I see now," he said to himself, mumbling under his breath. He raised his hand to the sky and made an oath: "I swear, I swear to all that is holy and good in this world, if my kingdom is restored to me, oh yes, if I get my revenge on that sniveling whisperer Nelcherath and that putrid Ockler, I will never partake of the accursed moss again."

"Never again!" he shouted.

Tharchelon's reverie was shattered as he suddenly tumbled backward, rolling all the way over in a backward somersault and coming up on his hands and knees. Damn hells, what had just happened?

He had fallen backward through the barrier.

No.

Not through it. *It was gone.*

With that realization he stood up and a wave of panic broke over him. The sun was still peeking over the western horizon. The barrier was down far too early! His advantage by a surprise nighttime raid was in jeopardy. Perhaps Nelcherath did not yet know that the barrier had failed? Could they wait a half hour more for the darkness before attacking?

No.

The murmuring traitor would discover it soon enough... if he didn't know already. Every moment of delay accrued to Nelcherath's advantage.

Things had not gone according to his timetable but... the barrier *was* down! *It was down!* His panic subsided. The joy of knowing it was gone was worth the price of bad timing. He could already taste the wonderful bitterness on the back of his tongue. He felt a slight smile cross his lips.

Rathenel raced to his side, a confused look on his face. "My King..."

Tharchelon cut him off with a bellowing voice. "Form up! Infantry in front... archers to the rear!"

"But..." Rathenel's protest was once again cut short.

"Make haste," Tharchelon said. Calmness and reassurance infused his tone. Rathenel turned and began barking orders.

They double-timed it across the open pastures and through the cover of the few small wooded areas between the fields. Most of his soldiers were recently pressed into service and were not in shape for such a run, but no matter, he drove them anyway.

The integrity of the battle formations had grown ragged and several of the archers were lagging badly. Some of the infantry were dragging their large shields on the ground behind them. It would be a miracle if he could get them reformed, but the driving need for haste outweighed everything. They had almost a mile to cover from where they started, to the large clearing around the great Bystle Tree. How long would it take them? Six minutes? Eight?

And what are you outlanders doing? he thought. *What are you doing with my moss? Are you waiting for me as I command-ed? Hoping to save your loud-mouthed little companion?*

Tharchelon shivered in delight. Yes, they must be waiting, waiting with the moss! Soon he would have his moss back, kill them, and reclaim the Moss Garden for his very own.

Tharchelon topped a rise and finally had a clear view of the Bystle Tree in the waning light. To his relief, there was no army arrayed against him to defend the tree. Perhaps Nelcherath was still unaware and surprise was still with them.

Then an unsettling realization... not a single fruit on the tree shone with its ever-present yellow glow. What did *that* portend? Was it a consequence of the children darkening the Moss Garden? Had they somehow betrayed him? Was something else at work that he hadn't expected?

He pushed the worry from his mind. He had but these few precious moments to seize upon any advantage that yet remained.

He issued new commands to his lieutenants. The advance slowed to a walk as his commanders shouted their orders. The soldiers slowly began to reshape into their proper formations. Three companies, each comprised of about a hundred warriors, arrayed ten by ten, marched before him; two companies out front and the third, comprised of his best warriors, behind in reserve. Each warrior was armed with at least a makeshift spear and several also carried a short sword or Rothkin dagger. Every third man carried one of the large shields they had been constructing with such fervor. Two platoons of fifty archers each flanked his command position behind the infantry.

With a nod to his lieutenants, they advanced, quicker, his men jostling and jogging raggedly. Tharchelon focused on the tree. He estimated it was three or four hundred yards away. He scanned the large exposed roots at ground level for signs of movement. It was growing dark and the distance was still too great, but his instinct told him that Nelcherath's forces weren't deployed on the ground... yet. He turned his attention to the branches. Once again, the foliage, light and distance made detection of movement difficult. At a minimum, there would be sentries in the branches. Were they aware of his invasion yet? Perhaps he was the beneficiary of the same darkness and distance? Perhaps total surprise was still on his side?

That's when he saw it; a glowing Bystle Fruit moved through the air around the south end of the great tree, then another behind it. Two Bystle Flyers, each powered by a glowing fruit. Why were these fruits still glowing when all the rest were dark? He didn't have time to think about it. The glowing fruits turned and were headed straight for him at high speed. His little army had been discovered.

As the flyers closed in, the archers on his right unleashed a volley of arrows. The first flyer evaded to the left and the arrows fell short of the second flyer. The gunner on the first flyer let loose a lightning bolt that struck very near his right front company. Undisciplined conscripts cried out and the formation lost cohesion briefly, until their barking commander regained control.

"Shields!" Tharchelon bellowed.

The commanders of all three infantry companies relayed the orders and the large shields began a disorganized dance to end up held overhead in an overlap that looked sloppy to Tharchelon, but created a somewhat functional cover from arrow fire. The lightning from the flyers was a much more serious concern; nevertheless, the shields seemed to buoy his troops.

His army pressed forward doggedly. As they advanced another two hundred yards, his archers were able to keep the two flyers somewhat at bay. He feared that more of the flyers would appear and scatter his force, but to his great relief, there were only these two.

He marveled at his fortune. He was depending on surprise and the cover of night to avoid the flyers, but when forced to charge in before darkness fell, his small force might have been annihilated by a force of more flyers. The lack of Bystle Fruits seemed like his first genuine stroke of luck in longer than he could remember. However disconcerted and unsure he felt about the darkened fruits, it was working to his advantage at the moment.

No sooner had he finished reveling than one of the flyers dived to evade a volley of arrows and flew straight at his left front infantry company, firing a lightning bolt directly at the front line. The ground exploded and he could see several bodies, and worse--body parts--thrown through the air. His left formation broke and scattered as the smell of burnt flesh and hair filled the air.

The situation would slip out of his control if he didn't get that formation back in a semblance of order. He desperately yearned for a pinch of moss as he raced forward angling left, and began shouting commands to the fleeing troops. His commanders followed his lead and moved to rally. Miraculously, the company reformed. A few cowards had managed to run off. Half a dozen more had been killed by the lightning strike, their charred and smoking corpses left behind. Some of the new conscripts stared at the carnage, fear etched on their faces as his small army continued the advance toward the tree. It would be a miracle if they held formation when things got serious.

They were now close enough that he could see some activity in the branches of the tree. Warriors also milled about the exposed roots on the ground. There was no longer any doubt; their attack was known. Had they arrived in time to attack before Nelcherath's forces were completely ready? Tharchelon fretted over his chances. On the one hand, he had achieved some semblance of surprise and the enemy had been deprived of most of their flyers. On the other hand, their attack was at dusk instead of night, and his army consisted of a sloppy force of mostly undisciplined farmers and sheepherders. The battle on the ground would be fully joined in short order. Even if all went according to his plan, there were still too many unknowns. Was Cael waiting for him in the Moss Garden at this moment? What if Cael had been captured and all this was an elaborate trap set by Nelcherath? A pinch of moss would clear his head and help him focus... eliminate his worries. The promise of moss drove him.

Nelcherath's archers began lobbing arrows and ballista fired javelins from their platforms among the high branches. The flyers finally turned away to avoid friendly fire and circled southward. His three infantry companies, two in front and one behind, slowed, their shields held above them forming a protective cover like a turtle shell, as they waded into range of Nelcherath's archers.

Tharchelon held his breath as arrows rained down upon his front ranks; a pivotal moment. Would his troops be protected and stay in formation as he hoped? Or would the withering arrow fire break them? Several excruciating moments passed, but his formations held! Tharchelon could hear the rapid fire thunk, thunk, thunk of the arrows as they accumulated on the upturned shields. His infantry ambled forward, looking increasingly like three giant porcupines.

Tharchelon could now see dozens of Nelcherath's warriors that had taken up defensive positions in the labyrinthine roots of the great tree, but a sudden flurry of activity was even more concerning. Enemy soldiers began pouring out the main entrance from the trunk. The moment of truth was at hand. He nodded to one of his adjutants, who blew a long note on his horn.

Though there hadn't been nearly enough time to thoroughly drill his troops, they reacted to the horn blast just as practiced. The front two companies charged the enemy line still forming up in front of the entrance to the great trunk, while the reserve company hung back, supported by one of his archery platoons. His own command position stayed far behind, just out of arrow range, with a few dozen warriors and the other platoon of archers for protection. The enemy archers high in the branches, for fear of hitting their own, directed their fire away from the front infantry companies, concentrating on the shielded reserve. An arrow found a small gap between the cover of shields and a soldier cried out. A few archers in the branches lobbed long shots his way, but they fell short.

Sounds of battle erupted as the infantry forces at the roots clashed. It was very difficult to tell what was happening. Two large knots of chaos frothed, ebbing and receding as the battle raged. His left company seemed as if it was being pushed back, but there was nothing he could do. He had to rely on his company commanders. Though Nelcherath's warriors were better equipped and trained, they were confused and leaderless. His left company faltered but held as the right company broke through and advanced, creating a thin gap in the enemy line. His reserve company suddenly charged forward, dropping their large shields as they went. Tharchelon was elated. His plan seemed to be coming to fruition! His mouth began to water in anticipation.

His reserve troops barreled toward the breach. The crucial moment in his plan of attack was at hand. If his reserve company could break through, Nelcherath's forces would scatter, leaving entry to the tree itself... and the moss... clear. His reserve company was just at the point of engagement when Tharchelon heard a trailing high-pitched scream. A sudden movement from the branches high above caught his eye. A glowing orb suddenly dropped from the gloom of the canopy above. It was a third Bystle Flyer plummeting straight down. He focused all his attention on it despite the urgent climax of the battle on the ground. The flyer was overloaded with passengers... *it was the outlanders*! He could see the big one spread-eagled across the back of the flyer, holding on for dear life.

His brain scrambled to make sense of what he was seeing; they should be waiting for him in the Moss Garden. Had they simply chosen to abandon the mouthy dark one to his fate?

That's when he saw Needle glommed on to the left wing. A slowly building rage accompanied his growing realization...

The scrawny bastard had somehow escaped and rejoined his companions, and together they had betrayed him.

Tharchelon had a flickering moment of hope as it appeared as if the flyer would crash straight into the ground but the nose suddenly came up and it straightened out, accelerating at a low altitude straight toward him. He saw Cael's face in the pilot's enclosure, clearly illuminated by the last glow of light bouncing off the clouds from the west. In a flash, he surmised the depth of treachery. Needle had a dagger clamped between his teeth as if he fancied himself some sort of ancient hero. Cael, finding himself free of the burden of abandoning his friend, had simply decided to take the moss. That must have been why the barrier collapsed and collapsed early. Cael had the moss... *all of it...* with him on that flyer.

His archers loosed a volley on the approaching flyer.

The battle on the ground forgotten, blind fury pushed his panic aside. He snatched a spear from one of the guards standing near him. Cael flew toward him in a slow bank, *gaining* altitude slowly. Tharchelon carefully timed the approach and took several running steps forward and hurled his spear off with great force.

Chapter Thirteen
Bad Moon Rising

"Without the protection of the guild or incredible luck, very few recently infected wererats ever survive long enough to learn to control their disease. Out of control and helpless to stop themselves, most are hunted down and killed. Others commit suicide when they regain their true form and realize what they have done. For those struggling to survive alone, the only hope is not found in their will to fight against what they are becoming, but instead in their surrender to what they now are; only then is there survival. In the meantime, the only respite from the ravages of the full moon is a cloudy night."

> \- Artemis Ovinko, Master of the Thieves' Guild of Taglyon

15th Day of Summer - 9:45 PM – Branches of the Bystle Tree – 15 Minutes to the Full Moon

Cael felt a surge of panic as the flyer began to plummet toward the ground. He had badly underestimated how much downward force he'd need to exert to keep the flyer airborne. The falling sensation overwhelmed every nerve fiber, ripping at the concentration required to right this fatal situation. He frantically gripped at the wooden rail in front of him. He wanted to scream but could not find the air in his lungs to do so. Brynn had no such trouble... her scream trailed over the battlefield.

The unforgiving ground rushed up toward him. Cael pushed directly ahead of him with his mind but that served only to slow the fall. It did nothing to right the flyer. Cael now pushed, not down toward the ground, but down relative to himself. It worked! The flyer's nose angled up. *Yes!* Cael was quickly form-ing an understanding of how to fly this damn contraption!

He continued to push the nose of the flyer upward so that it was parallel with the ground but they were still losing altitude. With a mighty heave of his mind, he exerted all the force he could muster downward and backward. His strategy worked. The flyer's descent slowed in earnest and started to move for-ward. They avoided striking the ground by perhaps a dozen feet and began to gain speed. They passed over a small group of Tharchelon's archers supporting engaged infantry units at the base of the tree. A few were alert enough to fire their arrows up at them. A percussive thunk, thunk, thudding sound reverber-ated up from the underside of the flyer.

Cael refocused the magical force down and back in an ef-fort to gain altitude and speed. Unfortunately, the flyer was de-signed to carry two diminutive Rothkin, not four large humans; especially not one the size of Bannon 'Mallet' Bygrave. Rather than gain altitude, they gained only forward speed.

Cael glanced back. All three of his companions were hold-ing onto the flyer desperately. The oversized Mallet gripped the base of the fruit spike in one mighty, white-knuckled fist and held the crossbow post in the other. Needle and Brynn were smashed together, legs akimbo, with Needle edged out at one of the wings. Brynn held the back of the pilot enclosure with one hand and Needle's forearm with the other. She had a gaping cut on her bicep where an arrow had grazed her. The siblings' faces were frozen in open-mouthed, bare-teethed terror, while Needle's face was etched with an unhinged kind of glee, the hilt of his silver dagger clamped between his teeth. Cael caught Needle's eye momentarily before the boy's gaze snapped up-ward. Cael instinctively followed Needle's glance.

Now out from under the canopy of oversized leaves, Cael could see the darkened sky. Needle, ever alert, was scanning for the full moon but the sky was mostly cloudy; not thick, rolling storm clouds but thinner ones with gaps here and there. There was a lunar glow from behind an opaque cloud. He flashed another quick look at Mallet, whose eyes were now ratcheted shut. Cael relaxed slightly; Mallet still looked like Mallet. Per-haps his demented metamorphosis was being held at bay by the cloudy evening? Cael glanced at Needle again, the dagger still between his teeth. The boy's eyes were now fixed on Mallet and Cael suddenly understood the dagger. Thankfully, the moon was veiled, at least for now.

Cael adjusted the force, pushing more downward and less backward, and it helped gain altitude. They had now climbed to twenty feet or so above the ground. Cael became aware of the sounds of battle rising up from behind them, where the main section of the fighting was occurring. Ahead they were approaching another line of Tharchelon's archers.

It was too late for Cael to react as they flew into another volley of arrows. An arrow deflected off the front of the flyer's nose near Cael and whizzed away into the dark.

In that moment, by the last fading light, Cael glimpsed the unmistakable face of King Tharchelon. He stood on a shallow knoll just behind the line of archers, looking straight at them. Their eyes locked and in that instant Cael felt a familiar haunting chill spread gooseflesh over his entire body. The madness in those eyes reminded him distinctly of the horror he had experienced in the Moss Garden. Tharchelon was not so far removed from insane whispers in the dark core of the Bystle Tree.

Cael slowed and desperately tried banking away from the king, but it was too late. Tharchelon reached out and grabbed a spear from a fellow warrior. He anticipated the momentum and direction of the flyer and heaved the spear with practiced expertise. For a brief instant, Cael thought the spear was coming straight for him, but it passed over his head.

Mallet bellowed. Had the spear struck him? A sudden dark thought ran through his mind. What if Mallet had been slain? What if Tharchelon had just ironically saved them all from Mallet's wererat savagery?

He craned his head around at the same time the Bystle Flyer inexplicably seemed to struggle to maintain altitude. What was happening? He could feel the magic of the flyer ebb distinctly. Mallet was fine... absolutely fine... but the Bystle Fruit on the spike was not. Tharchelon's spear had struck it, almost tearing it from the spike. Mallet was trying to cobble the large chunks of glowing fruit with his meaty hands in an effort to restore the globe to some semblance of its original shape. A rivulet of glowing juice dripped down his forearm.

"We got a friend," Needle yelled suddenly, looking back to the southeast.

Cael glanced back. It was no friend. A flyer had emerged from the canopy on the south end of the tree and was pursuing them. It was moving much faster than he could propel their own flyer. The exertion he had to expend due to the weight was taxing him terribly and they were slowing. He could still make out the shadowy edge of the treeline at the edge of the vale. In the deepening dark, it was difficult to judge distance, but perhaps they were a minute away... More? Less? Would the other flyer pursue them past the border of the vale?

A lightning bolt from the other flyer sizzled through the air at them, missing them by mere inches. Cael could feel the hair on his arms and the back of his neck stand on end.

"Son of Abyss!" Needle cried. "Can't you make this thing go faster?"

Cael looked back at the pursuing flyer. It was gaining on them quickly. He had flown them clear of Tharchelon's archers but the other flyer was just reaching them. It earned an arrow volley of its own.

Cael had not managed to gain any altitude since the fruit was damaged. It was hard enough just to keep from dropping. He felt the power of the flyer wane and he knew his options were few. The tall pines at the edge of the vale loomed ever nearer, but he didn't have the altitude to clear them. He banked to the left to evade the other flyer and desperately tried to gain altitude.

The enemy flyer banked with them and the gunner fired again. The lightning bolt left a white streak in his vision but was high and wide.

Cael watched the other flyer as it continued its banking maneuver long past any logical point. It continued to roll over and went headlong into the ground, impacting with a resounding and final crunch. Cael could only guess that their pilot had not been as lucky and must have taken an arrow.

"Anyone hurt?" Cael yelled over his shoulder.

No one said anything. He hoped that meant everyone was okay, and turned back to flying; time to get out of the clearing.

He tried to gain altitude at the expense of speed. The strategy seemed to get them to a safe altitude, but Cael would have liked to be going faster as they just cleared the pines at the edge of the vale. He pushed to increase the speed and suddenly the flyer dipped rudely. Cael's guts lurched upward.

Mallet cried out and Cael looked back. Mallet had fumbled the chunks of fruit he had been holding together and only a few fleshy glowing remnants clung to the spike.

"We're going down," he yelled and turned to face forward. Gripping the bar, he tried to use whatever magic was left in the flyer to bring it down gently, but that was a fool's hope. He dived down through the outstretched branches of pines that beat at the flyer. Using every mental facility he had, he kept the flyer level and, facing forward as the branches whipped against it, trying to send it spinning.

Thank the heavens, a small clearing appeared ahead. Cael became suddenly aware of the high speed at which they were traveling. It did not seem so fast from higher up, but with the ground as a reference, the rate with which they traveled was vomit-inducing. The image of the other flyer crashing zipped through Cael's mind. He was quite sure the two Rothkin on board did not walk away from it. Cael's mind blurred as he tried to search for any scrap of knowledge on how he might bring the flyer safely to the ground. His brain latched desperately onto a solution and Cael pushed forward mightily to slow their speed.

There was not enough magic left.

They struck the ground going fast... too fast, but at least the flyer was level. It skidded along the grass and weeds, vibrating violently. Cael felt helpless as the wooden boards began to crack, then splinter at the mercy of the forest undergrowth. Eventually, the furious forward momentum slowed and a shower of dirt kicked up into Cael's eyes and mouth as the flyer gouged down through the vegetation and into the soft, thick earth. With a great final lurch, the flyer came to a sudden halt. Cael heard a great snap . The post that held the crossbow broke free of its base and flew over his head, carrying Mallet with it, end over teakettle.

The dust settled. The dell was dark.

"Mallet," Cael whispered. "You okay?"

Mallet groaned.

Brynn disentangled herself from Needle and grimaced as she reached into her pocket, retrieving her sandstone. She stood and slowly traced the sigil upon it, providing a searing bluish light to the small clearing.

"Yeah, I'm okay," Mallet said finally as he rolled to a sitting position. Cael couldn't believe it. Most people would be severely injured or, gods forbid, even dead if thrown that far. But Mallet seemed mostly okay. What was once his tunic now hung in shreds, revealing a host of deep scrapes and cuts across his arms and torso. Mallet stood up, his knee giving a hollow pop.

"Brynn," Mallet called. "You all right?"

"Fine." Brynn ran her hands from the top of her head down to her feet, taking inventory of all the bumps and cuts but finding nothing broken.

"I'm fine, too," said Needle. "Thanks for asking."

Needle was also covered in a patchwork of cuts and bruises from the pine branches that had flayed them as they went through the trees.

"Tharchelon is coming," Needle said as he carefully crawled away from the flyer on all fours. "He started running after us when he threw that spear."

"We need to get out of here," Mallet murmured.

"What about the full moon?" Brynn asked as if she had suddenly remembered her brother's treacherous tie to that blue-white omen in the sky.

"It must be up by now," Mallet said, scanning the heavens.

Cael looked skyward. Luckily, there was still quite a bit of cloud cover, but Cael quickly located the soft glow of the moon behind a large cloud. It was dangerously close to peeking around the wisped edge.

Cael looked at Mallet. Mallet looked down at his hands, then looked from Brynn to Needle and back to Cael. "I seem okay."

"It must be the clouds!" Brynn said.

Needle said nothing, but Cael could see he held his silver dagger at the ready by his side, out of Mallet's sight. Maybe they would get lucky tonight but Cael doubted it... the cloud cover was not complete.

Suddenly, a huge beast swooped out of the sky. Cael recognized it from the aeries in Demon's Bluff as a Gryphon; an enormous winged mountain cat with the head of a buzzard. Its mighty wings beat furiously kicking up a swirl of dirt and pine needles as it alighted in front of them.

To their collective horror, none other than Wheizer Rhelbog leaped down from the back of the great beast, an insane smile spread across his face.

"Well, well, well," he said exultantly. "I expect you have something for me?"

As Wheizer stood staring at them with his death-black eyes, the full moon quietly slipped out from behind her flimsy cover. Its light shone down around them, bathing the entire area in its eerie glow.

Wheizer's grin morphed into a visage of unbridled ecstasy.

CHAPTER FOURTEEN
Full Moon Fever

"Witches partially understood that most ancient of eldritch languages: the void. No devil, no demon, no hell nor abyss could decipher that hoary magic of madness, yet these few fearless mortals made their thrust into the breach. A mere mark could hold power from the time before 'The Before'. It is no wonder that witches have long been known to practice in secret, which only adds to the viperous rumors."

> \- Return of the Cult of Yex, by Caed the Chronicler

15ᵗʰ Day of Summer - 10:00 PM – The Forest Outside the Vale - The Full Moon

Mallet looked up into the face of the full moon, balled his right hand into a fist and smote his chest; a warrior's salute of respect and a call to war. A war he had no chance to win, but a war he would fight, oh yes, he would fight. Hopefully, Brynn, Cael and Needle would have the good sense to get the hells out of here before it was too late.

His muscles tightened and spasmed as the full moon bathed him in its eerie glow. His dry mouth flooded with saliva, signaling the imminent onset of vomit. Down he went to one knee. Gripping his glaive with both hands, he avoided falling further. Pain slithered from the pit of his stomach to the core of his sacrum, up his spine and knocked on the base of his skull.

He locked his gaze on Needle. The Agrabi boy's eyes narrowed but did not falter as he backed away slowly, holding his silver dagger between them.

Wheizer stepped forward between Mallet and Needle. He raised both arms skyward as he basked in the moonlight, a look of rapture on his face. Wheizer began to shimmer like the heat rising from the desert. In mere seconds, he shifted into his hideous half-rat, half-man hybrid form.

"Now is your time, my son!"

Oh Father, Mallet thought. *Have you given me over to this creature? Am I no longer your son?*

The awful truth struck him fully. Dagorn had *indeed* forsaken him, and given him to Wheizer. If he remained useful at all, it would only be as a tool to his father's designs.

Another ripple of energy started from his tailbone, running up his spine and into his skull. Again... the burning sensation at the base of his skull...

He looked to Brynn, pleading for her to flee. They were both motherless... and now, fatherless. What were they now but orphans? And soon he would lose even her.

He gripped his glaive again... the change was assaulting him... and focused his gaze on Wheizer. That was the key. Kill Wheizer first. Kill his 'new' father and hopefully that would slake his thirst, or wound him enough to save Brynn and Cael... and even Needle.

"Run," he hissed at them.

But his companions didn't move a muscle. The fools!

"Fight it," Brynn pleaded.

"Come on, cheese eater!" Needle said, still holding forth his puny silver blade.

Wheizer's laughter echoed. "Ah Mallet, son... you can't win... trust me... give in to the sweetness and I'll make sure you don't kill your darling sister. She still has value." He squeezed these words through his mouth, dragging them out as if to saturate them with gleeful malice.

Mallet considered that offer seriously.

The ripples from his guts ran up his spine again and smashed into his skull, like someone was taking out a lifetime of frustration on his head.

The pain at the base of his skull flared into a symphony of vibrant sensations. Memories flashed through his mind, but he recognized none of them. He dropped to both knees, lost his grip on the glaive and fell face first into the rich forest loam. The smell and taste of dirt saturated his senses.

The whole glade seemed to fill with the moonlight.

Mallet had watched Wheizer shift that night two weeks ago in the mausoleum and had imagined himself going through the same transformation. He imagined the transformation of his face would be a blinding pain, but instead it was simply a tightening that started between his shoulder blades, making his skin taut. It felt like an invisible hand pulling his face back. Again, the pain thundered behind him. Vast quantities of saliva sluiced around his mouth, splattering over his lips and onto the ground.

"I can't win," Mallet tried to say, fighting to control his jaw as it worked open and close like a chattering monkey. No intelligible words came out, just a random slather of syllables. Could he feel his teeth elongating? Would he soon feel fangs serrating the inside of his lip?

The pain in his skull built and built. He saw lights every-where. Needle, Cael and Brynn were frozen. Even Wheizer was astounded, backing away.

He gallantly fought the pain one last time, trying to breathe it down his spine, but he couldn't hold it and his breath ex-ploded out of him. The energy overcame him, spreading up over his crown, down his face, throat, heart and settled into his stomach like a warm glass of milk.

Calm suddenly filled his entire body. He felt utterly beaten and surrendered into something much bigger than himself. There was something sweet about it and tears filled his eyes. Was this what Wheizer felt? It wasn't entirely bad, to be honest. He felt no lust for darkness, only a calm feeling of peace settling over him like a cool splash of water on a burning hot day.

Wheizer's euphoria gave way to confusion. "What?" he screamed. "Impossible! You are mine!"

Mallet grabbed his glaive and stood up.

"That whore denied me my son!" Wheizer screamed.

Mallet assumed the change was now complete and once again wondered at how different it felt than he had always imag-ined. He still felt no lust for blood. He *did* feel anger at Wheizer though, and his desire to kill him was still gratefully intact. He would definitely enjoy this murder and feel no remorse about it later. He gripped the haft of his glaive and took a tentative step toward Wheizer, testing his new form.

Wheizer looked up at the moon, his snout stretched back in a sneer, white teeth glistening with his own abundant saliva. He looked back at Mallet, then back at the moon.

"This can't be happening," Wheizer said, as wonder and dismay battled for supremacy over his features.

Well, of course it can be happening, Mallet thought. *You infected me, you should know.*

Wheizer turned and looked at Brynn for one brief moment, then bolted away.

The little bastard. He knew Mallet wanted to fight him, and fled so he would attack Brynn instead. So much for preserving his sister!

But he wasn't going to get away so easily. So fixed was Mallet's purpose he had absolutely no desire to kill his sister: Oh, no... it was Wheizer he wanted and Wheizer he would have.

He grinned and took off after him, crashing through the humid night air. Wheizer quickly reached the magnificent gryphon.

The beast reacted to Wheizer's command and launched itself up into the air, mighty wings beating and carrying him quickly up and away behind the boughs of the overhanging trees.

The scrambling sound of his companions filled the small glade behind him. Mallet stood with his back to them, staring up into the sky filled with thousands of stars and one very full, bright moon.

They had their chance. They should have run.

He took a deep breath, filled his lungs, let it go slowly.

Then he heard Needle speak: "So... he let the rat get away?"

Mallet shivered. He didn't want to turn around. He didn't want to kill his sister. He didn't want to kill Cael. Hells, he didn't even want to kill Needle.

What I want to do is run away, into the forest, and never look back.

"Mallet," Brynn said.

Why was she still here?

"Go away, Brynn," he warned.

"Mallet," she said, her voice softer, "I want to see you."

"I'm going to kill you," he said.

"No you aren't," she said. "I'm your sister. Turn around."

"Turn around ya, dumb cheese eater," Needle added drily.

Mallet wanted to run... but what if he *could* control it? What if Brynn was right? Should he run, or turn around?

"Mallet," Brynn whispered.

She was going to get herself killed.

He swung around and faced them.

The three of them stood staring at him. What was the look in their faces? It wasn't horror. He had expected terror, but instead it was... confusion? Awe? What was it?

Brynn came toward him, Needle followed. He flexed, gripping his glaive. How could she be so foolish?

"Step back, Brynn," he said in a low commanding tone.

She didn't listen. She just kept coming up to him, tears filling the bottom half of her eyes. She reached out and gripped his hand...

He looked down. Her hand held his. His normal... *human...* hand.

Mallet pulled away, touching his face. Ran his hand over his shorn scalp. He hadn't shaved since they were on the boat, and there was a fine dusting of stubble sprouting already.

But no wooly, greasy wererat hair. He felt his teeth with his tongue, same as they always had been. No sharp teeth. No elongated tongue.

"What's happening?" Mallet asked.

"What didn't happen, is what you mean," Needle said as he came up to stand next to him.

Mallet wrapped his mind around this impossibility. He had drunk the blood. He had been bitten. He should definitely be infected.

And he had felt the infection... it had been coursing through his body, but... something had stopped the transformation. He touched the back of his head, where a warmth lingered.

He looked at Brynn, but she sucked her breath between her lips.

Mallet suddenly heard a wild scrambling, scuffling, like the sound of a dog digging for a bone. They all heard it, and turned as one to face in the direction of the flyer.

"Holy hells," Needle breathed. The moonlight clearly revealed a rabid Tharchelon standing over a bloody and nearly unconscious Cael. He was stuffing moss into his mouth.

Tharchelon turned to them, the whites of his eyes snaked with pulsing red.

CHAPTER FIFTEEN
Moonchild

"Most memories fade with the passage of time. But those few memories that grow with time... those are the memories that shape the person."

- Ancient Buerdeleise Parable

15th Day of Summer - 10:15 PM - The Forest Outside the Vale – The Full Moon

> *Tharchelon transformed.*

It wasn't his body that changed; in fact, it wasn't physical at all. The very essence of his being, *his countenance*, transfigured before Mallet's eyes. It was as if he had been instantly crossbred with a demon, taking on the aspect of demonry, yet without any outward demonic trappings. What Mallet saw in Tharchelon frightened him more than the witchcraft he had feared all his life. It evinced something ancient and malign. He tried to swallow, but his mouth had gone suddenly dry. It reminded him of how he felt when the whispers in the Moss Garden had assailed him. A vertiginous abyss of darkness within Tharchelon leaked out through the coal glow of his eyes. That demon wouldn't be satisfied with a mere taste of moss. That demon had baser hungers. Tharchelon fixed on Mallet with an unmistakable lust for blood--*his* blood.

Mallet lowered his glaive slowly and, using the haft, gently moved Brynn and Needle aside like they were chess pieces swept from a board. A battle lust of his own welled. Mallet hadn't shape shifted as he expected was his fate, but perhaps the hatred of the wererat was still there? Or perhaps it was a murderous rage that came truly from within him? In either case, slaughter was in his heart and at this moment indulgence suited him fine. Hells, it would even do him good. He was just in the mood and killing this treacherous Rothkin king would grant a measure of satiety.

Everyone feared that Cael would fulfill the fourth prophecy and turn evil. Who knew? But Mallet had his own demons to fight, literally and figuratively it seemed. He hadn't turned wererat but he still worried about himself as much as Cael... maybe more so. For now, such worries were swept aside in favor of the moment at hand. Now he would focus that hole in his soul at someone darker than himself.

Tharchelon seemed to detect Mallet's eagerness. "It's mine now," he hissed, holding the bag of moss tauntingly as he stalked toward Mallet.

Mallet glanced up at the moon and once again became aware of the curious tingling on his back, the calmness rushing through him. *I am your orphan now, too,* he thought.

Mallet relaxed as Wheizer had trained him, feeling for his center and when the moment was perfect, struck with his glaive. The attack should have beheaded the little Rothkin... only it missed the mark... badly.

In one horrific flash of insight, Mallet realized that it wasn't just Tharchelon's appearance that had changed. His reflexes had become inhuman. He had moved so fast that it allowed the Rothkin king to avoid certain decapitation.

Tharchelon stepped in deftly, nullifying the reach of the glaive and lashed at Mallet. One hand clutched the pouch, but the other slashed across Mallet's shoulder, dragging dirty claw-like nails across the still inflamed pink scars that Wheizer had inflicted not two weeks earlier.

Mallet fell backward in surprise and Tharchelon came down upon him. The Rothkin's hand thrust out and grabbed Mallet's throat. The hand was far too small to constrict Mallet's massive neck, but he realized in a flash that didn't seem to be Tharchelon's plan. The little bastard latched onto his larynx with startling force, digging his filthy nails into his neck, intent on ripping his throat out.

Mallet reacted in a panic, swinging his left fist over in a

crushing blow to Tharchelon's temple. Any normal person would have been knocked out cold, but Tharchelon clung to Mallet's chest and kept squeezing his voice box, his fingers desperately trying to force their way through his neck skin to wrap fully around his larynx. A series of popping sounds emanated from his throat and reverberated into his ears.

Briefly, Mallet saw that Brynn and Needle tried to intervene in some way, but Tharchelon dealt them each blows with his other hand, still clutching the pouch of moss.

Cael cried *"Hold!"* just as he had done when he paralyzed Wheizer back in the mausoleum in Demon's Bluff. Cael must have recovered from the beating Tharchelon had given him in time to intervene. Mallet thought surely Cael had saved him. But whatever magic Cael commanded was rebuffed by Tharchelon. The Rothkin paused only to gloat. He stared at Cael and just laughed. Mallet took advantage of the distraction and hurled Tharchelon off his chest.

The Rothkin tumbled off but sprang to his feet. Mallet gulped for air. The little bastard had damn near succeeded in ripping his throat out; he would have been successful if he'd had a few moments more. His throat felt like he'd never swallow again. He tried to sit up. Tharchelon's claws had gouged the skin of his neck and blood flowed freely from the wounds.

Tharchelon approached in a crouch, clawed hand flexing eagerly, an evil leer twisting his hateful features. Mallet kicked at him but the Rothkin king dodged the blow and leapt back on his chest with inhuman ferocity. It reminded Mallet of a rabid sand badger he had once seen attack a cat. The cat had no chance...

Mallet punched up, using his superior reach to push Tharchelon away, but the Rothkin deflected the blow expertly. He pulled a knife from his boot in a frighteningly fluid motion.

Mallet knew immediately he was in trouble... he was not the badger in this fight. Mallet twisted himself to avoid the blow but Tharchelon was too quick. The blade slipped between his ribs on the right edge of his chest. Time seemed to slow suddenly as he felt the blade withdraw, accompanied, oddly, by less pain than he had anticipated. He felt a sudden flushing sensation pass over him. It was the same as when the full moon had first manifested itself. Was he transforming into a wererat now after all? Was the mortal wound enough to trigger the lycanthropic transformation at last?

Tharchelon raised his blade to finish the job. The knife plunged but Tharchelon's wrist was stopped short, caught in a mighty claw. Dust and wind filled the air, a high-pitched screech pierced Mallet's ears and Tharchelon jerked skyward and was suddenly gone.

From astride the gryphon, Wheizer winked down at him. Tharchelon dangled by his forearm from the beast's mighty claw. With three mighty beats of its wings, the gryphon gained a little more altitude and then flung the Rothkin away. Tharchelon tumbled through the air chaotically and was engulfed in a large patch of underbrush.

Being saved by Wheizer was barely preferable to dying at Tharchelon's hands, but at least Brynn, Cael and Needle had a renewed chance to escape now. He might be dead already considering the stab wound Tharchelon had given him.

Mallet scrambled backwards through the dirt and leaves away from the gryphon that hovered mere feet above him.

Wheizer issued a series of short, choppy whistles and the gryphon descended. Its hind legs touched down as it went after Mallet with the huge talons of its front claws. Its wings flapped furiously for balance kicking up dust and chaos. Mallet tried fending off the claws, but they clamped around him and he was caught as if he were nothing more than a field mouse.

"Ho! Valsipherus!" Wheizer called, and the gryphon's mighty wings began to beat harder in preparation to lift his heavy load. Mallet struggled, but could not break free. Mallet saw Needle standing behind the gryphon, looking indecisive. Mallet instinctively reached out his hands to Needle, as if the scrawny Agrabi could possibly be of any help to him. It was a ridiculous notion.

Needle looked him in the eyes and just nodded. There was a silver flash in the moonlight, and Mallet watched stunned as the Agrabi boy started to run. He jumped and landed on the back of the gryphon behind Wheizer.

Having himself just been stabbed, Mallet cringed as Needle drove his dagger into Wheizer's kidney. The blade came out as

Wheizer howled and began thrashing about. Again and again the blade flashed as Needle made the most of this moment.

Wheizer was strapped into his saddle and he could not easily maneuver around to get at Needle. He started twisting and hurling his elbows behind him in an effort to dislodge the Agrabi boy. The gryphon wasn't making it easy for Wheizer, as it was violently struggling to take off with the heavy Mallet in its claws.

Wheizer managed a loud-pitched whistle and the gryphon lurched up into the air as it dropped Mallet. A panicked look erupted on Needle's face with the sudden gain in altitude. He looked around frantically and put his hands on the back end of Wheizer's saddle and shoved himself backwards, barely avoiding another of Wheizer's flailing elbows. He lunged over to the bough of a looming pine tree, barely catching the branch under one arm.

Needle secured himself and started to climb down as the gryphon climbed skyward in the darkness. Wheizer was slumped forward in the saddle.

Needle dropped from the lowest branch and stood up grinning.

A screech echoed over the night sky. Wheizer was gone.

Cael stumbled out of the brush where Tharchelon had been flung by the gryphon. Mallet saw that the young wizard's clothes were torn, drying blood from scratches covered his face.

Mallet forced himself to stand, but it took nearly everything he had to do it. Brynn desperately tried to keep a bandage held to the side of his bare chest.

"He's gone," said Cael. "He took the moss..."

"Tharchelon?" Needle asked.

Cael slumped to the ground. "Give me a second. We have to go after him."

"Not before I find out what's going on," Mallet demanded. "What did Wheizer mean? He said, *'That whore denied me my son!'* What does that mean, Brynn? Why didn't I change?"

Mallet lowered himself painfully to the dirt. The full moon bathed them and the bloody clearing in bright light.

Brynn cradled him as he lay there, looking up at the full moon. She gazed down at him, searching his eyes.

She shook her head, tears filling her eyes. "Mother protected you... from him."

Brynn wasn't making any sense. "What? How?"

"She knew," Brynn sobbed. "She knew what he would try to do to you."

Mallet coughed for several seconds. He drew his hand back from wiping his mouth. His spittle was tinged with blood.

"She must have known from when you were just a baby. She must have done it when you were an infant," Brynn mumbled with a smile and a vacant look in her eye. "It's the only explanation."

"What in the hells are you talking about?" Mallet coughed again.

Needle appeared next to him. "You got a witch sigil tattooed on your back. A big one."

Mallet felt as if he had been slapped... he looked back at his sister. "That's impossible."

"You looked like you were about to rat out and then the sigil just appeared and lit up under the moonlight, flashing all silvery," Needle said it just a little too matter-of-factly. "Then you didn't change."

The memory of his mother... a witch... it all suddenly made sense.

"Mother did this to me?" he said and looked up at Brynn as he feebly reached behind his head, trying to feel the tingling place between his shoulder blades. It brought on another round of coughing.

Brynn could not stop crying.

"Now is not the time for this," Cael said.

In a rush, Mallet understood. He understood the truth of *everything*.

His entire life, he had been taught to fear witches and their wicked symbols. Little did he know all that time, his own mother had put one of those marks on him. Were there more upon him that he did not know about? The mere thought repulsed him. The memory of the night his mother had died flooded back in vivid detail. For over a year, he had not allowed himself to think about it, even for a moment.

Mallet was vaguely aware that his sister was bickering with Cael, but he didn't care. The memory of his mother dying on the floor was all-encompassing.

She had breathed her last breath and began to transform right before his eyes. Her unblemished skin had begun to change. Slowly, the faintest of blue began to appear in blotches all over her face, arms and neck. The blue blotches slowly darkened, turning from light to a deep, dark blue. The blotches grew and filled in. They connected to each other, forming swirls and impossible patterns. *His mother's body was completely covered with witch tattoos.* The hideous marks had been there, tattooed on her all along, invisible while she lived. When she died, whatever magic kept them unseen died with her, exposing the appalling symbols.

"But he's hurt, Cael," Brynn shouted indignantly.

Mallet didn't care what they were on about. It all made sense. His mother had tattooed him with the same invisible ink she had used on herself. Brynn was right. She must have done it when he was just a baby. There was no other way.

Mallet vomited. The revulsion of his own mother's tattooed face, coupled with the realization that he himself had at least one of those witch marks scribed into his very flesh, was more than he could bear. For all he knew he might be covered with them. He rolled over to his side and heaved again. A furious round of coughing followed. He spat blood upon the ground and rolled back, looking up at the accursed full moon.

Tears welled up in his eyes and rolled hot down his cheeks. He no longer knew who he was. His entire life he had lived with the surety that he was Bannon Bygrave, son of Dagorn. He was a Duke's son--heir of a noble family. He was destined for greatness. Everything had always been exactly as it seemed. This he had always known with the surety that the sun would rise in the morning and would set at night.

But no longer. His father was a slaver, perhaps worse. Dagorn assumed that he would simply go along. When he didn't, he had allowed... *commanded*... his wererat henchman to infect him to force his compliance. Mallet realized that he was nothing but a tool to his father... He was not a son. To make matters worse, his mother, whom he had always adored, turned out to be evil. She was a witch, and by the look of her tattoos in death, she had embraced her witchcraft with utter zealotry. His sister was infected with the same pernicious ideas that his mother espoused. Even he himself was not free of the horrible marks he so loathed.

Through his tears and coughing, Mallet was aware that Cael and Brynn were still arguing, but it did not matter.

He was not who he thought he was. Everything he thought he knew was a lie. His parents were a lie. What was worse? That his father had betrayed him to a wererat to advance his own business interests? Or that his mother had protected him from that betrayal with something just as loathsome? He was marked by her evil witchcraft!

He thought suddenly of the fourth prophecy. No wonder the Cult of Yex wanted him...

Who am I? He thought, as darkness dragged him away to a sweet, longed-for embrace.

CHAPTER SIXTEEN
Bravado

*"The purity of our intent is to serve Yex, our demon master; to bring him to the world to reign. The hardships on our journey are so many that we can but focus only on the next thing, the next step, the next battle. Each closed door, each obstacle, each fight requires untold sacrifice. If the price to be paid is to pluck out one's own eye; to cut off one's own limb; to sacrifice the lives of one's own family... that price **will** be paid, but the cost shall **never** be counted! It was by this means that we were able to obtain the Abyssal Moss as the hour grew desperate."*

- From the *Lich Diary of the Archmage Xylex*

15th Day of Summer – 10:30 PM – Edge of the Bystle Vale

Tharchelon slowed to a walk as he made his way through the forest, his senses honed to vorpal sharpness by the Bystle Moss. Damn hells, he wondered if he hadn't maybe taken too much? When the moment he had longed for lo these last many days had finally arrived, his anticipation overwhelmed him. The huge pinch he had shoved into his mouth had seemed a fitting reward at the time; the taste had been exquisite. But now his head was spinning. He saw colorful tracers dancing about vibrantly and an oddly pleasant fiery pressure was climbing up his spine and seemed intent on pushing his brain out of the top of his skull. His heart was beating like it wanted to escape the cage of his chest.

Damn hells, it was good to have the moss again!

But there was so little left...

His initial instinct was to go back and kill the kids that had caused him such grief... and he wanted to... oh, how he wanted to watch them die! The feeling of the moss had now focused his thinking and the fog in his brain vanished. He became aware of a new burning priority... *the crop of Bystle Moss must be reestablished.* Even to the exclusion of the kids or any other priority. The magic of the Bystle Fruits had failed completely, which was a worry in and of itself, but... by his assessment of the quantity of moss in the pouch, perhaps they hadn't harvested all of it?

He hoped that even a few strands remained... strands he could nurture and coax back into a strong crop. But what if it *was* all harvested? He had no idea how to re-establish a new crop. It would be a long, difficult and uncertain journey; separating out spores from the remaining moss, implanting them back onto the altar, solving the problems of light and water. There was no certainty the spores would even take.

It was all he could think about. He resented having such worries. It would be nice to have no cares... to be free to just enjoy the sensation. What if the pouch was all the moss there was left? If this was all the moss there ever would be... well... that thought just filled him with icy, black terror. Cold sweat broke on his brow. Perhaps the huge pinch was just about the stupidest thing he had ever done. He would have to limit himself to small, infrequent pinches that would draw out the inevitable conclusion as long as possible. And then what?

He had to get back to the tree. He had to get up to the Moss Garden and assess the situation. *What if he couldn't grow any more moss?* He broke into a run.

Soon, he emerged from the trees at the edge of the vale and into the last vestiges of the battle. He stopped, surprised. He'd been so intent on the moss that he had forgotten about the battle and that weasel Nelcherath.

At first glance, things indeed looked promising, but it was hard to know for sure. The light of the full moon was bright, but the customary light of the Bystle Fruits was absent. He shrugged off another pang of worry.

What appeared to be campfires burned here and there throughout the vale. Had his forces won the day? Were Nelcherath and the rest of the traitors rounded up? *Seditious bastards.*

A part of him wanted to stay and deal with them personally

but he couldn't afford to wait even a moment when the future of his precious moss was at stake.

A rider on a pony approached. Tharchelon tensed.

It was Rathenel!

"We've got our forces in the tree now, everything is being mopped up."

"Nelcherath?"

"We'll find him."

"Handle it. I'm heading in."

"You'll need a torch."

Tharchelon made his way purposefully through the passageways of the Bystle Tree. He found that he could make his way without a torch. His eyesight was sharp, and he could discern shadowy edges.

"I ordered them to wait in the garden," he muttered to himself.

The kids had indeed lowered the barrier as he had hoped. But they had defied him and tried to steal his moss. *His moss!*

They were emboldened to betray him because the scrawny dark one had somehow managed to escape. He reminded himself to discover who was responsible for that catastrophe.

He considered his luck as he walked. The kids had almost succeeded and escaped. Imagine if he hadn't seen them in time. Imagine if his spear had missed its mark and not brought the flyer down.

The gryphon and its rider were a mystery to him, but it didn't matter. He'd recovered the moss they had stolen from him and now he once again stood at the entrance to the Moss Garden itself. His moment of truth was at hand. Would there be any left at all to nurture?

A sudden fit of itching overcame him and he scratched vigorously with both hands. What in the damn hells was happening?

Had his first dose worn off so quickly? He had eaten so much. How long had it taken him to get back here? After crawling from the thicket where the gryphon had tossed him, he'd raced most of the way to the edge of the vale. True, he'd walked for a while after meeting Rathenel... an hour perhaps? Not much more than that if at all.

He couldn't need more already... He had to conserve what he had left in the pouch. But another dose would help him think clearly so he could reestablish the crop... wouldn't it?

Yes... another pinch is entirely justified.

He stopped and opened the pouch. He took a sharp breath. There was so little left...

He couldn't help himself. Colors flashed in his eyes and a ringing sound surged in his ears as he took just a tiny pinch.

Mmm... Mmm... The bitter taste was so good...

And the itching stopped! Thank the heavens, but his head was still swimming.

Never mind. He had to get into the Moss Garden.

The door at the base of the stairs failed to respond to his touch; another sign that portended calamity in the Moss Garden. The wood however, was seamed and he found it quite slack. He had little difficulty forcing a gap that he could slip through. *Worrisome.*

As he neared the base of the stairs, he had to stop and rub his eyes. He saw what he thought was the familiar yellow glow of the Bystle Fruit emanating from the top of the stairs. He paused and studied. It was not a hallucination... *it was real!* A sudden jolt of hope surged through him. The rest of the tree's lights were completely out... but there was light in the Moss Garden! It must mean that there was some moss left after all!

He was about to ascend the stairs when he heard the hissing whispers. He stared up the weakly illuminated stair and indeed he could see hints of almost transparent shadows dancing about. He had forgotten about the hissing shades. The last time he had taken so much moss, he had accidentally found his way into their realm... It suddenly occurred to him to worry. Something was different. They were wandering outside of their previous boundary and they were surprisingly loud. What was going on? Had some of them escaped their strange dimension? He considered the questions but none of the potential answers changed the fact that he needed to be in the Moss Garden.

Tharchelon licked his lips and took a few steps up the stairs. It was suddenly much cooler... colder even than an early spring rain. What was going on? This was beyond anything in his experience and he hesitated again.

It all seemed like an ill omen. Was there any moss left?

Worry about the moss propelled him as he slowly climbed the stairs. The hissing shadows swirled around him, almost as if they were clinging to him for warmth. He thought he could make out actual words contained within the whirlwind of whispers.

Redemptor...... restorer..... welcome..... salvation..... grandson....

He pressed on and held his breath as he arrived at the landing at the top of the steps. The first thing he saw was a single Bystle Fruit, previously picked, laying on the altar, glowing faintly. It was partially mangled and its yellowy juice dripped down one side of the altar in a glowing rivulet.

Was there any moss left?

The shadows danced and hissed about as he walked quickly forward, trying to ignore them... his focus was completely on the altar.

His heart sank. By the light of that single, faint, lonely fruit he could see that the treacherous children had not left him even a single strand.

"Seditious usurpers," he grated, fighting back tears of rage. "Liars and thieves..."

He reached out and ran his fingers over the rubbery red stubble. He shivered, hatred filling his body. He felt hot despite the cold, like he had a fever.

The whispers and shadows swirled about but suddenly amidst their rancorous din, he perceived a discordant note. His heightened senses picked it up... a heartbeat.

Two heartbeats.

He turned to see two of the traitors, Needle and Cael, stepping toward him with daggers raised to strike.

15th Day of Summer - 10:30 PM – Forest at the Edge of the Bystle Vale

Cael clenched his fists, feeling as if he were about to lose control. His arm ached from the wound in his hand. He clenched and released several times, trying to circulate the blood and reduce the pain. His face was bruised and swollen and combined with the scratches from the thicket, his face itched terribly, but scratching made it worse.

He had contended with Tharchelon since the moment they had climbed up from the gorge. He had railed against the Rothkin King with everything he had but it came to nothing. The rabid little bastard had ambushed him and beaten him bloody. Then he took the moss... snatched it right away.

I have to get it back.

He stepped back from where Brynn was cradling Mallet. He needed to think. Time was wasting and he needed a plan. He walked shakily back over to the wreckage of the Bystle Flyer. The damage wasn't really *that* bad. The crossbow mount had broken free, but the spike for the fruit looked fine. The condition of the flyer wasn't the biggest issue, however. The fruit that powered the damn thing was destroyed... torn to bits and strewn about in front of the flyer. Even now Cael could see the faintest glow still struggling to give light from the smashed and torn pieces.

Needle hobbled over to stand beside him, a strange, unhinged grin on his face.

Cael ignored him and turned, limping to Mallet and Brynn. Brynn cradled her brother's head in her lap. His eyes were closed.

Cael felt helpless. "Can you wake him? We have to get going."

"I already told you no," Brynn said loudly, flashing Cael a menacing look through her tears. "He's been stabbed, Cael! He's not going anywhere!"

"But Tharchelon is getting away with the moss!" Cael said. "Mallet is the toughest kid I've ever known. You saw him keep going before, even when he was torn to shreds by Wheizer."

Brynn looked dumbfounded, but Cael pressed on, trying

hard to make his voice sound rational. "We have to get that moss back, Brynn, and I don't think we can beat Tharchelon without Mallet."

"It's over, Cael!" Brynn hissed vehemently. "It's gone and we aren't going to get it back."

Cael stared right into her eyes and said: "We *will* get it back. It's the whole reason we came and we aren't leaving without it."

"You don't even know why we need it," Brynn said, anger rippling across her features.

Mallet let out a whistling cough and opened his eyes.

"I can damn sure tell you that we can't let the cult have it."

"You're obsessed," Brynn accused him.

"Obsessed?" Cael threw her words back at her. "Are you out of order? Do you think maybe, at minimum, we need to keep it out of the hands of lunatics like Tharchelon, Wheizer and say, someone like your father? You know what it can do... if we can't take it from them, we have to destroy it."

Brynn shot him a look to kill, and turned back to Mallet.

Cael took a deep, calming breath, centering himself like his grandfather had taught him. "Look," Cael said to Mallet, "I get it. You're hurt and you're dealing with... a lot of questions, what with a sigil being on your back and all, but--"

"It worked," Needle interrupted. "It protected your dumb ass from ratting out."

"That's not what I was going to say," said Cael. "We need your help now, Mallet. We *have* to get the moss."

The state of Mallet's fugue was such that Needle's verbal prod and Cael's cold logic didn't elicit a response. Brynn's eyes were filled with tears.

Cael looked up at the sky and the full moon. "I'll go myself then," he said starting toward the vale.

"I'm going with you."

It was Needle. The scrawny Agrabi had surprised him. He would have expected Needle to exhibit his trademark fatalism and side with Brynn. Cael smiled at him.

"But we'll never catch up to him now," Needle continued. "He has too much of a head start and will beat us back to the tree. I think we'd likely get caught before we even found him."

There it was, Cael thought. The cynical Needle he had expected.

"I know where we'll find him," Cael said. "He's going to the moss room, I'm sure of it. We snuck in there once, we can do it again. We have to try, Needle."

Needle shook his head. "We have to get ahead of him."

Cael's frustration was about to boil over. He turned, ready to unleash on Needle... then he saw the dung-eating grin on Needle's face.

Needle bent down and picked up the leather sack he'd been carrying since he saved them from the attack of the flyer at the base of the tree. He untied the opening and reached inside.

To Cael's utter amazement, Needle pulled out a large, glowing Bystle Fruit.

Needle tossed it into the air and caught it. "I ain't walking."

Cael rushed over to the flyer as Needle followed. Needle pierced the glowing orb on the spike as Cael began strapping himself into the pilot's enclosure. He put his hands forward and grasped the bar. He could feel the slippery Bystle Magic coursing through the flyer. Good old Needle!

Brynn left Mallet and came over to them. Cael was certain she was going to argue again and he was in no mood for it. They had little time to waste.

"I think this is a mistake," Brynn said with resignation in her voice as she ignored Cael and gave Needle a long hug before he climbed into the gunner's seat.

"Just me and you," said Cael to Needle as he lifted off the ground.

Cael and Needle landed on the same platform in the Bystle Tree from which they had departed. Fortunately, the platforms and catwalks were completely deserted. If they had been spotted as they flew in, it wasn't evident. There were no shouts of alarm or other indications that they had been seen. The full moon had been obscured by the clouds for long enough for them to fly through the vale and Needle had smartly covered the glowing fruit with his tunic to hide their approach.

It was much darker under the canopy than Cael had anticipated. Had it not been for the ambient glow of the fruit that leaked out from Needle's tunic and Needle's sharp eyes guiding them, he might have wrecked, sending them falling to their deaths.

The battle was over. In the darkness it wasn't clear who had won, but in his heart Cael knew that Tharchelon's forces had been victorious. Ironically, he needed them to win. That was the only way he could be certain that Tharchelon would be back in the Moss Garden. If they had lost, Tharchelon might be captured or worse, might not have returned to the vale at all. They may never find him in that case.

Cael had considered that Wheizer might still be out there circling on his gryphon. But if he had been, they hadn't seen him and he obviously hadn't seen them, either. Cael doubted that Wheizer was still a threat after the vengeance that Needle had done to him. For all Cael knew, Wheizer might even be dead.

Cael pulled the glowing fruit off the spike, keeping it wrapped in Needle's tunic. It wasn't glowing as brightly as before.

"Why'd you do that?" Needle asked.

"You see any other fruits glowing up here?" Cael asked. "No point in leaving a reason for somebody to come investigate. Besides, if it's dark out here, it's dark in there." Cael made his way back across the catwalks to the trunk of the great tree where they had emerged earlier that evening.

"How we going to get inside?" Needle asked.

"We are gonna have to figure that out," Cael said grimly.

In the dim yellow light that peeked through gaps in Needle's tunic, they could see a vertical seam in the bark. Cael took Tharchelon's ring from a pocket in his robes and slipped it over his little finger, then pressed it to the wood near the seam.

Nothing happened.

He half expected that. With the moss harvested, the tree

had lost its source of arcane power. The thought reminded him... he reached out to feel for the *Arcanus Navitas*. It was incredibly thin... far too sparse to gather, but it did seem to be returning, albeit very slowly.

Needle reached out and pushed on the trunk just to the right side of the vertical seam and, to Cael's surprise, it yielded with ease. He got a quick glimpse of the darkness within. A chilled waft of air struck them and Cael almost dropped the ring as he was slipping it back into a pocket. Needle, also surprised, pulled away and the wood of the door flopped back into place as if it had been made of limp rubber.

Some quick experimentation showed that they could easily hold the gap open... much more easily than Mallet had done when they escaped from this spot. Cael guessed that the tree must have still had some magic left when Mallet had forced the door open before. Now, several hours later, it had none.

Cael stared into the darkness and cold beyond the gap and suddenly remembered the shadowy whispers that had assailed him within. When they had left here before, he had the moss with him. He had assumed that he would never again have to enter this place. But now he stared into the inky blackness beyond and realized that in order to take back the moss, he would have to face the terror of the hissing shades again.

"What in the abyss are you waiting for?" Needle whispered.

"Just give me a second," Cael shot back. He had desperately wanted to have Mallet along, but not even mighty Mallet would be able to protect against the insidious shadows. He looked into the cold darkness again and imagined that he heard the distant clanking of chains. He was sharply reminded of fishing with Danilus on Lake Balankov far to the south of Demon's Bluff when he was a child. Danilus had errands to run in Balankov, and Boxxaway had permitted Cael to tag along.

When the work was done, Danilus managed to wrangle a small row boat and they headed out onto the magnificent desert lake nestled among the narrow sandstone cliffs to do some fishing.

In the afternoon of the first day, they had come upon a series of wooden buoys floating in a wide circle around a section of shallow, dangerous rocks.

"Why don't those buoys float away?" Cael asked, curious.

Danilus rowed them over to one. "Take a gander under it."

Cael leaned over the boat and grabbed the buoy. He tilted it sideways and what he saw froze his blood. Attached to the bottom of the buoy was a metal chain, crusted over with barnacles and green algae. It descended from the buoy until it disappeared in the blackness.

Nothing in Cael's life had prepared him for the feeling of seeing that chain descending down into the depths. He squeaked, and fell back into the boat.

Danilus hooted with delight when Cael explained his reaction. *"Chains wrap round your soul... and drag you into darkness!"* he sang an ancient rhyme meant to frighten children. Cael realized his terror at seeing the chain wasn't rational, but his reaction had been visceral and terrifying nevertheless.

The part that haunted Cael the most was Danilus' phrase *drag you into darkness....* His imagination obsessed on what lurked below.

The fear of the chains and dark water had stuck with him ever since and at this moment, standing at the open entrance to the tunnel down into the Moss Garden, he felt the same terror he had felt when he first saw that chain.

And drag you into darkness...

"Can you hear that?" Needle asked, breaking the silence. His voice always rose in pitch when he talked about Wheizer or other things that frightened him, but here he seemed perfectly calm. "I think those whispers are still in there."

"You think?" Cael said. He could hear the hissing that he knew waited for him within. He felt flushed despite the cold radiating from the gap. For all his boldness in marching here to get the moss back, he hadn't really stopped to consider the ramifications. He hadn't stopped to consider the horrors he'd have to confront.

And drag you into darkness...

Had one of the distant whispers said that? Or had he imagined it?

"C'mon, Cael," Needle said as he pushed past Cael and opened the gap, stepping one foot across the threshold. "Hand me that fruit."

Terror climbed up Cael's throat as he fumbled the large fruit over to Needle. He was relieved to let Needle go in first.

Needle took the fruit and stepped through the gap into the tunnel. Cael imagined chains surging out of the darkness to wrap round Needle's soul and drag him down.

But nothing happened. He heard the hissing in the distance down the stairs more clearly, but no chains appeared. Needle set the fruit down just inside the opening and unwrapped it. The dim yellowy light seemed much brighter in contrast to the pitch blackness within. Needle quickly donned his tunic and picked up the fruit, holding it forth.

After five paces, Needle turned around and signaled. He even smiled.

Cael took a deep breath and stepped through the gap. It was easier to do with Needle now illuminating the way. He pulled out his dagger--the same dagger Boxxaway had given him--the same dagger that murdered his parents.

It was indeed unnaturally cold as Cael walked behind Needle. He pulled up even with him at the edge where the spiral stairs began to descend. Cael looked down into the inky blackness below and gripped the hilt of the dagger tightly.

He was reminded of another story Danilus had told him on that very same fishing trip on Lake Balankov. It was the story of a man sailing on a journey from Taglyon to the eastern kingdoms with his new bride. As they stood at the rail watching the waves pass by, the tentacle of a kraken rose out of the water and snatched his new bride off the deck.

And dragged her into darkness...

The man was so determined to save his bride that he instantly leapt into the sea to battle with the great monster, armed only with a knife as he swam down into the crushing depths.

"Would you have done it, Cael?" Danilus asked lazily that evening, smoking a pipe with his feet up on a sandstone rock as they sat around their campfire. "Would you been brave enough to have dove in after that kraken with only a knife?"

Cael hadn't answered, not sure anything could make him do such a crazy thing, especially after having seen that chain descend into the inky depths of the lake.

And drag you into darkness...

Needle nudged him with his elbow. Cael broke from his memory with a shudder. Cael gripped his dagger and stared past the light of the glowing fruit into the inky black depth of stairs descending to the Moss Garden, where lurked his kraken.

He forced his muscles to move and began to descend the steps.

"Those whispers followed you when you came up, didn't they, Cael?" Needle asked.

Cael just nodded.

"What are they?" Needle asked.

"Spirits, I think. Twisted, evil spirits trapped in some type of shadowy dimension in the Moss Garden... held there by the power of that moss."

"So they're free now?"

Cael shook his head. "I don't think so... but cutting the moss weakened the veil between them and us."

Cael remembered all the horrid creatures he had imagined as a child. The monsters lurked in the dark depths of the lake where the chain descended. He shuddered.

"Is that why it is so cold in here?" Needle asked.

Cael thought about that for a moment. "Yeah... probably."

They descended the stairs slowly, the light of the Bystle Fruit cutting through the gloom. The hisses slowly grew louder as they descended. The hair on the back of Cael's neck stood on end. With every step down they took, Cael's terror grew.

Soon, they came to where the spiral stairs landed and turned into the long straight stairway down to the Moss Garden. Cael hesitated.

"What's wrong?" Needle asked.

"This place is creepy, that's all."

"You remember Ganger's tomb?" Needle inquired. "That place was the worst... all those zombie rats."

"We got to hurry, before Tharchelon comes back," Cael whispered.

"Hey, I'm not the one stopping all the time," Needle whispered back. "You weren't afraid in there?"

"Where?" Cael asked, puzzled.

"Ganger's tomb," Needle hissed.

"Yes, of course I was afraid, Needle." Cael said. "I just didn't show it. We have to hurry."

"Okay," Needle said, louder than Cael thought prudent. "You're showing it now. Truth is, this place creeps me out, too."

Suddenly, the whispers below began to increase in intensity, like a nest of hornets that had been disturbed.

Cael clenched his teeth. They'd been heard. He would have been furious with Needle except for the fact that he knew this moment was inevitable. Whatever these spirits were, they were angry. He'd taken their moss and they wanted it back. Only he didn't have it. He looked down the long, dark, descending stairway and he knew what was coming.

Out on the rowboat with Danilus on Lake Balankov, his child's imagination had run wild. It had all been triggered by the immediate and primal terror he'd felt at seeing the chain descending into the dark depths of the lake. For the rest of the trip he couldn't stop thinking about it. He just knew all manner of huge lake monsters lurked below, waiting for the right moment.

A huge scaly creature swam deep down below and noticed the outline of their pathetic rowboat on the surface, silhouetted against the daylight. Looking over the edge of the boat, Cael saw a gargantuan shadow from below rising up to their boat at incredible speed. He was frozen with terror as the indistinct shadow ascended toward him, its features becoming more distinct as it approached; its huge glowing eyes and a massive maw opening as it rose. The creature expelled a gigantic air bubble that preceded it before it struck. Danilus' only warning was the bubble's cavitation under the rowboat. A rotten stench assailed them just before the massive jaws of the creature closed up around them *and dragged them into darkness.* Danilus had barely been able to calm him and row him to shore, so badly had he panicked himself.

The hissing shadows from below rose up and enveloped him.

Cael stiffened, unable to react as the susurrating mob swirled around him. He felt the coldness and malevolence of the shadowy horde reaching through the thin wall between the dimensions... trying their best to extinguish his life. As before, he sensed hundreds of independent tormented beings but of one mind and singular purpose. As they boiled about him he could once again catch individual words from among the lunatic jumble of whispers.

Returned... pockets... thief... find... atone... where...

"C-C-Cael!" Needle cried in terror.

Cael couldn't respond. The Agrabi boy was on his own. The tortured souls continued to churn about him. He could feel them slithering through his robes. Goose bumps erupted over his entire body as the chilling spirits assaulted him.

Gone... wasted... moss... disaster... missing... consumed....

And as quickly as they had arrived, they were gone. The shadowy mass descended back down to the Moss Garden. Cael realized he had been holding his breath and exhaled in a rush.

"What in the abyss just happened, Cael?" Needle asked breathlessly.

Disheveled as he was, Cael instinctively knew the answer. When he had climbed up the stairs earlier this evening after shearing the moss away from the stump, he'd thought the malevolent shadows were after *him*. But that wasn't truly the case. It was the *moss* they wanted. They lusted after it. It was their sole obsession. They had chased him before because he carried the moss. Now they had found him without it, so he no longer merited their attentions.

"I think they are looking for the moss, Needle," Cael said.

"And we don't have it," Needle whispered. "I'll be damned."

Cael had a sudden insight. He didn't know why he hadn't thought of it before. He knew all the pieces of the puzzle... he'd just never put them together. He knew that Xylex had sent Elija here to safeguard the moss. He knew that Elija had been instructed to teach his sons to do the same. If Elija had done exactly as Xylex instructed, it could mean only one thing. Elija was Tharchelon's ancestor! These spirits were the countless generations from then to now, connecting Elija and Tharchelon.

Cael felt a sudden sympathy for these poor, tormented souls. They spent a lifetime tending a deadly herb and it had affected them deeply, probably without them even knowing it.

Upon their death, they were drawn to the moss and were imprisoned by the irresistible longing to stay close to its influence.

Children in Demon's Bluff were taught about the horrors of the Abyss; the countless hells populated by unspeakable demons who ruled over the souls of the iniquitous for eternity. Surely the torments of the Abyss itself were nothing compared to the torture endured by the departed spirits of Tharchelon's ancestors; forever trapped in eternal yearning for that which they could not have.

The moss garden was eerily empty. Cael had half expected to see the bodies of one or more dead Rothkin lying where he imagined they had died in the chaos after he cut the moss, but there were none. Not even a single arrow or spear remained. Needle's single, fading Bystle Fruit illuminated the room including the now dark Bystle Fruits hanging from the inward growing branches above. The wooden altar, shorn clean of moss, occupied the center of the round room. The opening to the hall and stairs leading downward was on the wall opposite the one from which they had just entered.

The air here was extremely cold and the shadow creatures hissed and whispered as their indistinct shade forms danced about the place. Whatever their intent before, the shadows were now heedless of their presence.

"How long before he gets here do you think?" Needle asked.

"Soon, I expect," Cael said. He could see his own breath as he spoke. In all his life he had never been in a place like this.

"I don't like the idea of just waiting here."

Neither do I, Cael thought.

Cael went to the altar. Not a shred of moss remained. He put the fading Bystle Fruit upon it and walked over to the wall to the left of the entrance.

"I get it," Needle said, managing a scant smile. "Tharchelon comes in, is distracted by the fruit... and *BAM!* We attack him from both sides."

"Simple plan is the best," Cael said.

"You gonna be able to cast a spell here?" Needle asked.

Cael knew the answer. The greasy Bystle Magic that the moss had exuded was utterly absent now. If any of the *Arcanus Navitas* had managed to seep back inside the tree, he was not able to detect it. They had very few options against Tharchelon. Only surprise was on their side.

"I have my dagger," Cael whispered to himself, gripping the handle tightly once more. He thought again of the man who plunged into the depths after his cherished wife with only his knife, against a monster he could never hope to defeat.

And drag you into darkness...

Cael slumped to the ground amongst the incessant whispers and waited with his back against the wall. He shivered in the cold, trying to ignore the hissing. He barely kept his exhaustion at bay. How long had he been awake? He realized he hadn't slept for well over a day. Indeed, he'd been so anxious as they sailed up the river the night before they got to the switchback trail, that he'd barely slept at all. They'd started the climb sometime after midnight, almost twenty-four hours ago. He'd slept only a few fitful hours in the last two days.

He focused his thoughts on Tharchelon. The little Rothkin was going to arrive soon, and he was going to be hopped-up on that moss. They would have to strike quickly and cleanly.

Cael imagined him arriving, heading to the table. He could hear his footsteps and his breathing. The king was consumed with the idea that all the moss was gone. He stood there, hunched over, staring at the table, his body frozen with anger and rage, shaking ever so slightly.

Cael stood up, trying to be as quiet as possible. He tiptoed up behind the king. Tharchelon's back was to him. He had his dagger in his hand. This was the depths. This was the deep place at the end of the chain and Tharchelon was his kraken. Cael was the man who dove in with only his knife.

The king was still consumed with the altar, touching it with his fingers and muttering under his breath. If not now, Cael considered, when?

Cael.

Cael.

He startled awake.

"What the abyss, Cael?" Needle said from the other side of the room. The boy sat with his knees drawn up, shivering in the cold. "Wake up, for hells sake."

Cael looked over at him. He must have fallen asleep and begun to dream.

At that exact moment, they both heard the sounds from the stairs below. The shadows swept down the stairs in a congealed mass.

Tharchelon had arrived.

Tharchelon came into the room exactly as Cael had dreamed. He went to the altar. He touched it with his fingers and muttered to himself. Cael and Needle went after him. Tharchelon turned to face them as Cael raised his dagger. Down it plunged. Needle stabbed frantically as Tharchelon screamed in a frenetic, backpedaling retreat. Cael felt certain he had managed to stab the Rothkin King but was unsure of where. He saw a flash of blood on Needle's blade, and hope surged in him for a moment.

Tharchelon's shoulder and forearm bled freely as he fell backwards onto the altar. Steam rose from his seeping blood as if his soul was escaping his body. Tharchelon, either ignorant or uncaring of his wounds, bounced right back up and attacked Cael.

With frightening speed, Tharchelon moved in and punched

Cael, impacting his cheek with startling force which sent him flying backwards, arms windmilling until he hit the back wall, slamming his head on the hard wood. Cael slumped to the cold floor.

Cael dimly noted that Needle attacked the wounded king from behind. The two fought, scrambling and shouting, with Needle giving ground as he backed up toward the altar.

Cael realized he'd dropped his blade and started feeling around madly with both hands; his vision was blurred from the back of his head hitting the wall. The fingers of his left hand fell upon something odd, a wire...

He picked it up, confused for a moment until he realized it was the

Lorgnettes. They must have been knocked out of his pocket when he fell...

Needle hopped backwards, landing on the altar, the glowing Bystle Fruit between his feet. This enraged Tharchelon all the more, who scrambled after him. The fruit went spinning and the shadows weaved around in a crazy dance. The hisses rose to a cacophony of utter indecipherability.

Cael, for the first time since leaving Demon's Bluff, was at a complete loss. He felt utterly useless and out of options. Nothing had gone right, not a single thing since they had arrived at the top of the gorge. Except for maybe that Mallet's mother had protected him with that sigil on his back... But even that was meaningless if Mallet died from his stab wound. If Mallet were here, they would have a chance against Tharchelon.

If only he had some power, *any power.* Even a little. He was a wizard, for hells' sake! He didn't know how to fight with a knife or a pair of damn spectacles.

He looked down at the *Lorgnettes* in his hands. He had a sudden thought: was it possible to siphon power from them? He didn't think so. In fact, he was sure he couldn't. They were useless.

So, what then?

The fruit had fallen behind the altar and the floor around him was enshrouded in shadow. He kept feeling about for the dagger and at last his left hand found the warm pommel. He snatched it up.

Cael stood up. An ache raced through his skull as he did so. His wounded hand ached almost as much. He felt dizzy but standing up off the floor, at least there was more light from the glowing fruit. Cael looked down at his own hands and finally his eyes focused. His left hand held the peculiar jumble of wires and lenses: the *Lorgnettes*. In his right hand, he held the dagger. The Cult of Yex symbol was visible on the pommel through is fingers. He looked back at the *Lorgnettes* then again to the dagger. Remembrance overpowered him.

Once again, he was in the closet in the small room of Boxxaway's cottage in Demon's Bluff. He looked out through the gaps in the planking of the ramshackle door, at the birth of a child... *his* birth. Once again, he felt himself push the door open and attack. Once again, he saw himself kill his own father.

And then he was looking down at his own mother's face. He paused, trying to freeze time in those brief few moments where his mother was smiling tearfully, a sheen of sweat on her angelic face, as she held him for the first and only time.

And then he raised the knife in his hands. His hands! He recognized them. With his own hands he plunged the knife down into his mother's breast.

Something slammed into his body, knocking the *Lorgnettes* from his hands. He returned to awareness and by the faint light of the Bystle Fruit lying on the far side of the room, he saw that it was Needle that had collided with him. Needle's body collapsed in front of him, face hitting the floor. Needle still held his silver dagger, the gift from his father, clenched in his fist. His eyes were open, staring blankly as a trickle of blood ran from one eye down his cheek like a tear.

Needle was dead.

Cael's heart beat wildly as anger and terror filled his soul with utter despair. He had dived into the depths with his knife to face his kraken. He remembered more about that night around the camp fire at Lake Balankov. Danilus had ended his story about the man and his bride but Cael had complained that the story was not finished. So he asked the obvious question. "What became of the man and his bride?"

"They were never seen again, of course. Eaten, I reckon." Danilus had said bluntly. "You can't kill a kraken with a puny knife."

Tharchelon approached slowly from across the room with an eager bloodlust in his eyes.

Cael knew he was moments away from sharing the fate of the man and his wife... Needle's fate. The kraken would consume them all. The Rothkin King was far faster and stronger than he. He could not win.

You can't kill the kraken with a puny knife.

Tharchelon came at him. Cael swung with his puny knife anyway. Tharchelon was too fast and blocked the blow with ease. He stepped in and punched Cael in the guts several times with inhuman strength. The dagger slipped from Cael's fingers as his legs turned to rubber. He slumped down and sat upon the ground, certain that Tharchelon would finish him momentarily.

You can't kill the kraken with a puny knife.

Tharchelon stepped back to lord over him. "You think you can defy me and not pay the price?" Flecks of spittle punctuated his angry demand.

Cael knew he was about to draw his last breath. If he was going to leave this world, he decided he would leave it with his most cherished memory in his mind. Tharchelon could not take that away from him. He concentrated on the memory of his mother's smiling face as she held him... her newborn son.

"Don't think I won't hunt down your other two friends as well," Tharchelon gloated. "I'll find them."

Cael focused on the memory of his mother. Tears ran down

his bruised, swollen cheeks. Cael looked down and watched a tear fall to the floor, almost in slow motion. It impacted the wooden floor with a *thip* sound.

The sheen from the sweat on his mother's smiling face... the *Lorgnettes*... the droplet hitting the wooden floor...

He looked down at his hands.

His hands.

His hands!

Cael reached over and took Needle's dagger from the dead boy's hand and drew the blade across his left wrist in a swift motion. Tharchelon stopped short, bewilderment on his face. Then the Rothkin king laughed. "No need to kill yourself, boy... that's my job."

Time seemed to slow to a crawl for Cael. He watched as blood welled from the wound on his wrist. The fresh gash was very near to the angry scar from that morning those many days ago when he first tried Blood Magic. It seemed an eternity.

Cael watched the first droplet of his blood break free from the cut and fall to the floor to mingle with its sister fluid. Several more followed in a downward cascade.

As the drops of his blood fell, Cael felt a surge of magic flood his being. It filled him to overflowing with a thaumaturgic might more intense than he could have imagined.

The dagger slipped from his grip. It clattered on the floor and came to rest by Needle's face. Cael stood up and watched as his own arms raised and his palms turned toward Tharchelon. He heard a cry of effort and pent up rage emerge from his throat.

Tharchelon's expression turned from bewilderment to terror. Cael directed an unseen force of wild and unformed eldritch energy from his open palms, impacting the Rothkin king square in the chest. The force of the blow lifted him into the air and knocked him clear across the room against the far wall.

Cael knelt down by Needle in the few moments he'd bought himself with the Blood Magic. Tharchelon stirred against the far wall. Cael was disoriented, dizzy and hurt, but he still brimmed with a measure of magical power. He had to escape the kraken and he had to rescue his companion. His instinct was to take Needle's body and try to run out. As he grabbed the Agrabi boy around the shoulders, Needle blinked and his bleary eyes tried but failed to focus on Cael.

By the hells... *Needle was alive.*

Cael heard another sound and though he was momentarily filled with relief, he looked up with terror and saw that Tharchelon was standing up, gasping to regain the breath that had been knocked from him. No push spell or puny knife was going to kill this kraken. Cael knew he had to buy more time. But how would he be able to save Needle?

Cael stood and faced the Rothkin king. He raised his palms and decided this time he would take an extra moment and shape the magic he still had left.

Tharchelon sucked in a desperate breath and looked at Cael with genuine fear. Then, inexplicably, he looked askance at the glowing bystle fruit lying at the foot of the altar.

Cael suddenly felt a surge of genuine hope. Tharchelon was afraid of him! The first Blood Magic empowered spell had truly frightened him. And that wasn't even a proper spell. Cael had allowed it to explode from him unrestrained. A properly formed spell might indeed deliver a killing blow. Did he have a large enough reservoir of Blood Magic remaining? He focused on the simmering feeling within him and his confidence grew even more. *A knife would kill this kraken after all, but not in the way he'd imagined!* He took a last moment to finalize the formation of his spell. He would unleash the Blood Magic in a concentrated blast that the king would not survive.

He fired his spell, but before it struck, Tharchelon simply... vanished.

"Where in the holy nine hells did he go?" Needle mumbled, raising his head weakly and wiping blood from his nose with his forearm.

Cael's spell had surged from his outfacing palms in a focused torrent aimed where Tharchelon had stood a split second before. The spell detonated against the wall in a momentary shockwave of greenish flame and smoke. A crater of splintered wood remained when the magic dissipated.

Cael felt the sudden hollow absence of having depleted his entire reserve of magic at once... he could feel his very life force leak away with the casting. A wave of exhaustion made him gasp for breath as he slumped to one knee. He thought of his grandfather, aged beyond his years.

Cael struggled back to his feet, stumbled and nearly fell forward. He was completely drained; his legs felt weak and rubbery. Needle looked like he was almost on death's door. It was a miracle that he was still alive.

"Did you kill him?" Needle groaned.

"I don't think so." Cael shuffled over and retrieved both daggers. He slipped his own dagger into its sheath. "He disappeared before my spell was cast." He flipped Needle's silver dagger over and caught it by the blade and handed it hilt first to Needle.

"So where is he then?" Needle stammered, looking around.

That was indeed the question, but for the moment, Cael had become distracted by the roiling mass of the hissing shadows that were hugging the floor where Tharchelon had disappeared. To his amazement, the pouch was laying there in the middle of the milieu.

Cael's heart felt like it was trying to pound its way out of his chest as he raced over and snatched up the pouch, quickly opening it to peer inside. The hissing and turbulence of the shades increased as he did so. It was too dark to see clearly, so he felt with the end of his fingers and sure enough, he could feel the rubbery moss inside.

"Woah..." Needle breathed. "He dropped it!"

"I knocked it out of his hands," Cael said triumphantly, noticing that the shadows on the floor were starting to drift up to where he held the pouch. "We did it, Needle."

"Shouldn't we get going?" Needle asked as he struggled to sit up.

"As fast as we can go," Cael replied as he turned to survey the stairs. He had a sneaking suspicion where the Rothkin King might have gone, but what it meant was another question. "I am worried that Tharchelon might--"

As if to confirm his worry, a popping noise reverberated off the wooden walls of the Moss Garden. The blood drained from Cael's face as the abjectness of their predicament hit him.

Tharchelon reappeared from nowhere... accompanied by none other than a badly mangled Elija Abel.

Minutes Earlier

Tharchelon was momentarily dazed. The wind had been knocked from his lungs by the force of Cael's magical assault. The boy had managed to take him completely by surprise. He stood up, dizzy... trying to breathe. He'd hit the wall hard with the back of his head.

Needle regained consciousness as Cael was shaking him by the shoulders. The scrawny whelp should be dead.

Cael stood up. The intent in his eyes was clear. He aimed to kill him and after what he'd just done to him, Tharchelon didn't doubt Cael could do it. He had to escape. He wouldn't make it if he tried to run.

The whirling shadows roiled around his feet. Of course!

Cael raised his hands up menacingly, palms facing him. The boy had a murderous look in his eye.

In desperation, Tharchelon focused on the feeling of the moss that still bubbled inside him and was finally able to suck in a lungful of air. He unfocused his eyes, and concentrated on the glowing Bystle Fruit on the floor. A popping sound echoed in his ears and the floor lurched violently under his feet, then... calm.

All color was gone... everything was now varying shades of gray. This place was much brighter than he remembered. The Bystle Fruit on the floor next to the altar emanated weak shadow.

Cael and Needle were gone, too... no... not gone. He could barely see their forms. They were a distorted translucence... very faint. He'd done it! He'd used the feeling of the moss effervescing inside him to slip back into the strange dimension he'd visited before. He'd thwarted Cael, for the moment at least.

The shadows, now sharp and distinct, churned at his feet, hugging the floor. Tharchelon's immediate reaction was to extricate himself from the mass of shadows for fear they would attack him like the last time he had come to this dimension. But unlike the last time, the shadows did not molest him. He stepped sideways away from the mob of shadows, expecting them to follow him, but they stayed in the same spot. They seemed to be fighting one another as they hugged the floor.

Tharchelon looked around and found this shadowy dimension very much like he remembered it, with a major difference. When he had been here before, this place had been completely enclosed with no exits; just a round room with an altar in the center. But this time there were two exits, one leading to the stairway up and out, and the other leading to the stairway down, where he had entered. Curious, Tharchelon walked over to one of the exits. Sure enough he could see the stairs leading down, just as he would have expected. He turned to walk over to the other exit. Something was... a shiver raced up his spine and gooseflesh sprouted all over his body. It was as if someone had pulled all his excess skin taut. Someone was there, not an incorporeal shade like the ones that dwelt in this place... someone *real*. A flash of pale skin and black greasy hair turned the corner. None other than Elija Abel stepped out from the opening.

His appearance was terrifying. He was massively muscled... larger and stronger than Tharchelon remembered him, but his entire chest cavity was caved in. His skin was split in places and Tharchelon could see blackish streaks of Elija's dried blood. Intestines and other organs dangled through gaps in his skin and a broken bone protruded here and there. His weird, deformed hand was now crushed, but still the long, mangled digits moved as if of their own accord.

Elija limped toward him, his long greasy hair swaying as he moved.

"You disappeared after the obelisk fell on you," Tharchelon said haltingly. "I thought you had died."

Elija stopped directly before Tharchelon. "Death would have been... welcomed," he rasped after several more awkward seconds had passed.

"You came back here?" Tharchelon asked.

"I did not choose to come here." He looked in the direction of the hazy outlines of Cael and Needle. Cael had moved over to where the mob of shadows swirled around the floor. "I presume you still know what to do," Elija said, reaching out to take Tharchelon's hand.

Cael could not make himself move. Elija's sudden reappearance with Tharchelon was an utter horror. *Impossible.* They had defeated Elija. The obelisk had crushed him and the sunlight had finished him. *He... can... not... be... here.*

Cael took two dragging steps backward. He was desperately short of breath and it felt like all the blood was rushing away from his brain and toward his guts.

For the briefest moment, Cael had allowed himself to think they had won. Needle was badly hurt and all his magic was spent. Cael had given all he had to give, but it wasn't enough.

Tharchelon smiled in wicked triumph as Elija approached. Cael stepped in front of where Needle was still sitting to protect him. The futility and absurdity of that act was obvious, but he did it nonetheless. He stood between the monster and Needle, clutching the pouch of moss to his chest.

Elija continued toward him, his greasy, black hair swaying in time with his awkward limp. The injuries he bore from the obelisk only served to amplify Cael's terror. Even the crushing weight of the obelisk had not been able to stop the freak. Tharchelon's evil grin ripened into demonic rapture.

Elija raised his partially-crushed mutant hand and balled it into an oversized, horrifying fist. It may as well have been a sledgehammer, for Cael knew it would deliver a killing blow. He had no defense, yet stood defiantly. He decided that in this, his last moment, he would neither flinch nor cower.

Elija hesitated. A bright light burst forth from behind Cael. Its bluish beams cut through the waning yellow gloom of the sole Bystle Fruit.

Elija recoiled and stumbled backwards. Tharchelon's villainous smile slowly morphed into a look of confusion.

Cael turned to see Needle standing up, holding Brynn's stone, the sigil upon it blazing forth with intense blue glory.

About One Hour Earlier

Needle reached for the railing, ready to climb onto the flyer.

"I think this is a mistake," Brynn said with resignation in her voice. Needle blushed as she came right up to him and hugged him.

"Here," Brynn whispered in his ear. She pressed something into his hand. "It will be dark in there."

It was her ensigiled sandstone. He slipped it into his pocket as he climbed into the gunner's perch.

Elija backed away in horror, desperately trying to use his raised arms to shield himself from the light. A guttural howl erupted from his throat.

Needle limped forward next to Cael. He held the shining stone before him, directing its light toward the undead monster. Elija howled again as the light seared his upheld arms. Black smoke lifted off his skin and Cael smelled acrid death as Elija stumbled further backward. Tharchelon looked down at his own flesh, equally bathed in the blue light to make sure he was not similarly affected. He was not.

Every muscle in Elija's body strained like over-taut rope on the verge of rupture. Elija's ethereal scream turned into a ripping sound, followed by a loud pop. Inky black smoke flashed outward then dissipated quickly, like cooling steam.

Elija was gone.

Tharchelon's look of confusion turned to fury. His eyes locked with Cael's and he began to walk slowly forward.

Panic seized Cael as the king approached. Tharchelon reached forward intent on grabbing Cael by the throat and choking the life from him.

Cael raised his hands defensively and suddenly realized he was still clutching the pouch with both hands.

Tharchelon broke eye contact with Cael for a split second and glanced at the pouch of moss. An inspiration flashed into Cael's mind...

With both hands he tossed the pouch into the air. Time slowed as it sailed in a long arc over Tharchelon's head.

The murderous rage on the king's face turned to enthralled desperation. His hands, which were aimed at Cael's throat, shot upward, stretching to catch the pouch before it sailed out of his reach.

Cael jerked the dagger from its sheath and lunged forward.

The king's mesmerized look turned to horror as Cael plunged the blade deep into his chest. Tharchelon staggered back, the hilt protruding from his sternum. The Cult of Yex symbol on the hilt glinted in the blue light of Brynn's stone. Tharchelon caught the pouch of moss and pulled it down to look at it. His kraken's gaze drifted to the knife piercing his heart, then back at the pouch of moss in his hands as he fell backwards onto the floor.

Tharchelon was dead.

EPILOGUE

Cael pried the bag of Abyssal Moss from Tharchelon's life-less grip. The look on Cael's face was fading quickly but it would forever burn in Needle's memory. For a fleeting moment, Cael looked maniacal... drunken with power. Needle couldn't help but think of the chilling words of the fourth prophecy:

The Apprentice will stand at the precipice of the abyss and evil will beckon unto him. The voice of the first disciple shall cry from the dust unto him, and he will fulfill his destiny and will answer the clarion of evil.

he shall turn to evil, and with his companions, usher in the reign of Yex upon this world.

Needle watched Cael retrieve his dagger and wipe the blood off on Tharchelon's tunic. He sheathed the blade and moved to Needle's side. Cael gave him a gentle smile, put his arm around Needle's waist and helped him hobble to the stairs. Needle had no idea how they would escape, but he knew they would. Some-how, someway, Cael Hotheway would lead them back home.

By the light of Brynn's sigil stone, Needle noticed a shock of hair above Cael's left temple had turned white.

- *Return of the Cult of Yex,* by Caed the Chronicler

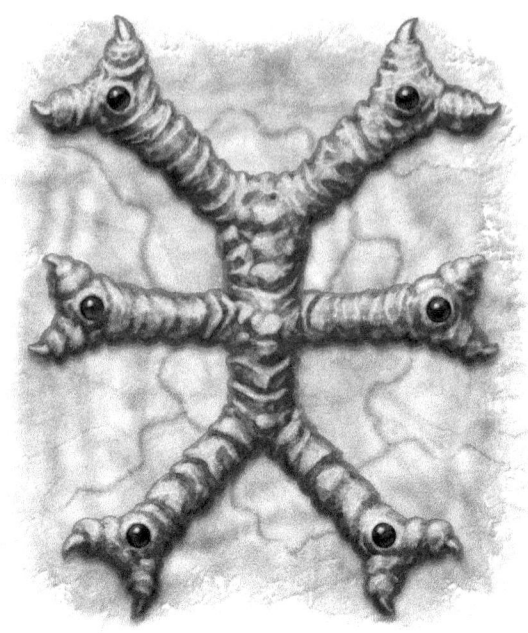

The story continues in:

Cult of Yex Saga: Part IV

Dear Reader

We sincerely hope you enjoyed Bystle Vale. If you did, please consider leaving a review on Amazon or another book-seller's platform. Each review helps us spread the word to other readers.

And if you get a chance drop by www.CultofYex.com or our Cult of Yex Facebook Page. Say hello make a connection. We love to hear from our readers.

AUTHORS NOTE

You hold and presumably just read the end of the first arc of the Cult of Yex saga. If it feels like a larger connected work, that's because it is. The first three novels were written as one very large novel, and due to size considerations were split into a trilogy. The end of Bystle Vale very much closes what started at the beginning of Second Cataclysm.

We are currently hard at work on the next arc of novels.

ACKNOWLEDGEMENTS

We have to thank everyone who read and commented on the novel, including: Matt Mecham, Asher Smith, Brittany Witt, Parker Webb, Raegan Garlitz, Mary Garlitz, Carol Archer, Dave Reed, Sheriece Farr, Shane Farr, Megan Bangerter, Tyler Barnes, Kaitlin Jones, and Peter Jones

Thanks to Jeremy McHugh for the art and Jennifer Leigh for the copy editing.

About the Authors

Jason F. Smith

Jason F. Smith lives in the beautiful mountains of Utah with his wife, three children, and menagerie of furry family members. Jason finds a great deal of pleasure as well as a host of ideas on his daily walks through the winding mountain paths, and is an avid lover of the magical art that we call "life".

C. Parker Garlitz

Parker is a 14th Level Nerd / 9th Level Small Business Owner, who lives in the beautiful mountains of Utah with his amazing family. Parker's fondest wish is to not be multi-classed and focus on adding more levels exclusively to Nerd. If you liked what you have read, you can help him achieve that goal. Tell your friends about the Cult of Yex.

www.ingramcontent.com/pod-product-compliance
Lightning Source LLC
Chambersburg PA
CBHW060219180626
46813CB00007B/2885